BOOKS BY SKOOT LARSON

The Lars Lindstrom Zen Jazz Mystery series:

> The No News is Bad News Blues
>
> The Real Gone Horn Gone Blues
>
> The Dig You Later Alligator Blues
>
> The On the Road Again Blues

The Dave Holman "Texas" Mystery series:

> Copkiller
>
> The Texas Detective
>
> The Pachyderm Predicament
>
> The Ivory Coast Puzzle
>
> Johnny's So Long at the Fair

Political Humor

> Apollo Issue, a Humorous Look at Healthcare
>
> The Palestine Solution
>
> The Testament of Jessica Crystal

Fantasy

> King Irv's Big Adventure
>
> King Irv's Cabernet Caper
>
> King Irv and the Holy Grail

King Irv and the Viking Marauders

a King Irv Fantasy Adventure

by

Skoot Larson

ISBN: 978-0-692-12228-0

Skoot's
Jazz
Books

First printing

For my granddaughter, Lindsey Cate Campbell, who is doing graduate work at my old school, UCSB. I'm so proud of you, Linds!

King Irv
And the
Viking Marauders

Part I
The Northmen Cometh

🐉 CHAPTER ONE 🐉

Hershel, King Irv's faithful Merlin, was being sent on a mission. Queen Sophie wanted her daughter, son-in-law, and granddaughter, all to be present for a celebration of her fortieth birthday at Warehouse Castle. Hershel had argued that his time machine had a limited capacity, and could only carry two people, max, and maybe a child as well if the two people weren't too heavy and the little one sat quietly on someone's lap.

Years earlier, Hershel had invented a time travel machine in which he'd gone forward and established a connection between King Irv's time and future England. As a result, King Irv's only daughter, Judith, had fallen in love with a man from the future, married him, and gone forward through the eons to live with him.

Sophie put her foot down. "Hershel, you *will* bring all my family together even if you have to make a dozen trips to the future to do it."

"Well," the Merlin had replied, "I can probably do it in two trips, highness, but who do I bring here first? And do I need to bring a lot of other stuff with them?"

"Some tins of strong ale for his highness would be nice," her ladyship smiled, resting her chin on the palm of her upturned right hand. "You know how King Irv loves that tinned ale from the future. And a few toys from those distant times to keep my wonderful granddaughter, Tiffany, amused. I'm sure she's too sophisticated to be entertained by the king's tabby cat or that animal's balls of bright red yarn."

Bird, King Irv's orange and white cat, pulled a face at this statement. What could be more entertaining to a child than a ginger tabby cat and a ball of scarlet string?

Hershel put a knuckle to his forehead in salute and wandered off to search for King Irv. He was pretty sure his monarch would laugh at the idea and tell him to go on about his business. He had so much piled up on his work bench at the moment. If the queen wanted to celebrate with her family, why not just let him take her to the future to see them all? King Irv wasn't that into parties anyway, no need for him to be there.

But when Hershel found his king, sitting out in the sunshine overlooking the ninth green of his golf course, Irv was in a romantic mood. "If having a big garden fete here will make m'lady happy," he told his Merlin, "then a big garden fete it shall be. Surely it isn't *that* much trouble to make a couple trips forward to bring everyone together."

"Sure, Irv," Hershel protested, "but then I gotta bring them back again as well... four trips in all! Maybe six, how much does your granddaughter Tiffany weigh? She's bigger every time I visit that future time." King Irv's daughter, Princess Judith, had married an Oxford scholar from the future. The princess, her husband, and daughter, all lived in future England, sixteen-hundred years away and near the famed university. "Do you know how taxing all this time travel is on me?"

"Oh please, Hershel," his king chuckled. "I secretly know you enjoy all this stuff. Every trip through time you make, you meet new people from God knows where. You can't fool me. Besides, on each trip you make, you can spend an hour or more in that public house you keep talking about, what is it? The Fawn and Firkin, I believe you called it. I know that you find their bitter ale to be superb and the bar maid who serves you as well." The king held his hands, palm up against his chest, as though cupping a pair of breasts, and winked at his man of magic.

Hershel turned a bright red as he bowed to his king. "Point taken, your highness," he mumbled. "So how soon should I have my machine ready to go?"

"Well," Irv chuckled, "Sophie's birthday isn't until next week, the 29th of September, so you've got some time to plan the trip."

Bird the cat materialized from nowhere, leaped into the king's lap and began purring.

Hershel smiled and nodded, although he felt somewhat resentful. He'd been planning to take his time machine on another little jaunt west to Marin County in California, just north of San Francisco, to visit Melissa, a lady he'd met when he'd been procuring Cabernet grapes for the Manischewitz brothers to make wine for the queen.

"You can count on me, highness," he told King Irv with a disappointed countenance and a half-hearted salute.

CHAPTER TWO

Queen Sophie's birthday party turned out to be a marvelous affair. Entourages from both their neighboring kingdoms were in attendance. Irv had, of course, expected his daughter-in-law's family from the next-door Kingdom of Vaude to be in attendance, but he was surprised by the large group of well wishers who came over from Berten-on-Cherwell, the monarchy to the west, who hadn't always been on such good terms with the Wholesale Kingdom.

Irv's son-in-law, Rutherford, had arrived a couple days early from future England so he and Irv could get in a round or two of golf on the Warehouse Castle's magnificent 18-hole course. Rutherford was always telling King Irv that the *old* course, which had been modeled on a plot from fourteen hundred years in the future, was much more pleasant due to the pastoral setting of King Irv's surroundings.

Now, as the party wound down, both men smiled as they teed up to start another game. Bird the cat lurked in the woods near the tee. He knew his monarch would not be safe without feline protection.

The foursome included King Irv's son, Prince Sol, and Rabbi Weiss, the kingdom's spiritual leader. Each man got off a good drive down the first fairway, although Rutherford's ball had hooked slightly toward the woods north of Hershel's Merlin cave and just short of the green.

Rutherford had strolled over toward the rough to find his ball when he caught sight of a group of blond-haired, red bearded men in tin helmets walking his way through the forest that flanked the golf course in the direction of the North Sea. The men had wooden shields slung over their shoulders and fat iron swords hanging from the belts of their tunics.

Thinking that he might be suffering from hallucinations brought on by too much time travel, Rutherford ignored the men and went on about using his eight iron to put his ball closer to the green. He hit his ball solidly, then watched to see if he'd been able to get near the flag with his shot. When he was sure he'd saved himself a stroke, Rutherford stepped off towards his fellow golfers.

He didn't notice that the bearded, helmeted men were following close on his heels, swords drawn, their shields now balanced on their left arms and raised. Some of the men carried stout iron hammers. Rutherford *hadn't* noticed, at least until he approached the green and saw that his golf partners were retreating with fearful eyes. The king's ginger tabby was standing stiffly with his back arched and red fur up on end, spitting towards Rutherford.

"What'cher?" Irv's son-in-law called, then he turned to see the large men following in his wake.

Rutherford thought back to the classes he'd taken in English history and did some quick math calculations in his head as the Viking men surrounded him.

"You're about 500 years too early," he told them. The Vikings gave Rutherford a confused look, their heads tilting slightly, but their swords and shields still at the ready. Rutherford tried to remember some of the Norwegian he had learned at university where he'd known a few students from that northern land.

"Tillike tidlig," he shouted, "Tidlig!" "You're too early!"

One of the men reached an index finger under the edge of his tin helmet and scratched his head. The men continued to dance a circle around Rutherford, swords raised, wearing bewildered looks. Finally King Irv took a brave step forward to introduce himself. "Hello, can I help you? I'm the king of this realm."

The Viking men quickly shifted their confused attention to King Irv. Rutherford, thinking quickly, translated, "Konge, vår konge." "Our king."

At this, the Viking soldiers took a step back, lowered their shields and bowed to King Irv. They understood about kings. They hung their swords back on their belts. One red-headed man who seemed to be in charge came forward, went down on one knee and bowed his head to Irv, then he stood up and started gesturing with his hands. He pointed to his men, then cupped his hands in front of his rather protruded stomach and pushed them out, like a ship moving forward on the sea. Then he gave a confused look, waved his right hand around his ear. Something crazy happened. He raised his knee and bumped his hand-clasped boat against it, then spread his arms wide to indicate the landscape of the Wholesale Kingdom all around him.

Hershel had strolled up from his cave at the sight of these strange men dressed in furs, leather and metal. He was the first to get it. He tapped his king on the shoulder. "Highness, I think these men were sailing their boat and something crazy happened landing them on our shores." As the Merlin spoke, he repeated the sea captain's gestures. The Viking chief vigorously nodded 'yes.'

King Irv, ever the good host, held out a fist as though it were wrapped around a glass and tilted it towards his mouth.

"Maybe we can learn more over a drink," he told his Merlin.

When the Vikings widened their eyes in understanding, Irv also gestured bringing his hand to his mouth and chewing. He then motioned the strangers to follow them towards Warehouse Castle, where there waited both food and drink. The golf game was quickly forgotten. Bird the cat, with a change of heart, stepped forward and rubbed his head against the lead Viking's furry boots.

CHAPTER THREE

King Irv cracked open a fresh keg of ale and passed pewter mugs of the brew around to his new guests. There were a lot of words offered by these hearty Northmen, but no one understood a single one. The Rabbi tried addressing them in Hebrew but to no avail. Hershel attempted to reach them with his limited Italian, but only received blank stares for his efforts.

As they were all standing and drinking ale with silly looks, Princess Judith wrapped her knuckles on the side of the drawing room door. "Father?" she called, "Do I hear someone speaking ancient Icelandic? Who are these people? And where did they come from?"

"That's what we've been trying to figure out," Hershel called out to her. "We found them out on the first fairway. They just kinda came strolling out of the woods."

"Hilsen fyrener," the princess called, turning towards the small knot of Northmen. "Har det seile fra Islandet?" "Have you sailed here from Iceland?"

Again, the leader put a finger under his helmet to scratch at his forehead. "Eesland?"

Princess Judith though for a minute, trying to remember the language course she had taken at Oxford a few years previously in modern time, many years into the future from where she was now standing. Then she let loose a string of foreign words and the Vikings all scrambled to answer her. Irv could make out occasional words like 'Saint Olaf' and 'Christian.' He thought he heard 'ship' and 'sea' somewhere in there. Eventually, the Princess settled into a conversation with the Viking's leader. When they'd finished, she turned to her father.

"Papa," she began. "These men have quite a strange tale to tell. They say they set sail from Norway, someplace called Hardangerfjord. Their leader is called Thor the Mighty. They aren't sure what the year was, but Olaf, one of their kings, had just been made a saint by some new religion from the south. They sailed southwest to escape the new religion and landed here, but 'here' seemed very different from 'here and now.'

"Near your castle, which lay in ruins when they first landed, they found a half buried rusting pile of tin. There was a bright square of crystal which caught their eye, protruding from the top of this pile, and when they tried to pull it loose it was attached to a small box with a knob on it. Thor's men took this box, along with the crystal thing, back to their ship."

Hershel the Merlin got a strange look on his face hearing this. "No," he breathed. "My time travel thingy, tell me this ain't so."

Bird the cat jumped into the Viking called Thor's lap and began to purr loudly, as though the man was his long lost best friend.

Princess Judith silenced the Merlin with a look, then continued her tale. "They were anchored in a nice sheltered harbor for the night right off the coast of where they'd found our old castle ruins. Thor placed his new prize in the center of their longboat, fastened to the base of the mast. No one knew what it was, but the crystals were beautiful and all his men were in awe of their new treasure.

"Then, sometime in the night, one of the sailors got curious. He apparently twisted a knob on the thing…"

At these words, Hershel gave an audible groan and rolled his eyes back into his head, looking as though he might pass out at any minute.

"The Viking men felt a weird sensation," Judith continued, "like their ship might be spiraling into the sky. When the spinning stopped, they opened their eyes to find they were still in the same small harbor, but the shoreline before them was somehow changed, it looked different."

"Oy vey!" Merlin whispered, holding his head in his hands. "I should'a known something like this might happen."

Princess Judith shot the man of magic another silencing look, then continued. "They decided to come ashore and look for the place where they'd found the crystal thing, to research if it was connected to something else or to discover just what it might be."

Thor called forth in a long string of his own language and the Princess translated. "Thor says he thought it might be a powerful magic that could drive these Christian southerners from his home shores. He wanted to bring it back to Norway to confront these Christian folk.

In the background, Hershel softly wept.

Then Thor pushed King Irv's cat off his lap and stepped forward, gave a slight bow to King Irv and said, "I know words of English. I learn from sailor." With that he turned back to his crew, touched one man on the shoulder and let fly with another string of odd words.

Irv and Hershel looked to the princess for an explanation as the Viking who Thor had touched dashed outside and was gone.

"Knut has been sent to relieve one of the sailors guarding the ship," Judith translated, "Someone called Miles."

Thor smiled and nodded his head saying, "Miles English sailor. Speak English good."

CHAPTER FOUR

While they were waiting for the return of the Northman known as Miles, Queen Sophie called for the cook to bring a platter of cold beef that their guests could eat. The queen was shocked when her guests ignored the good cutlery and linen serviettes she had set on the table for them and simply grabbed handfuls of greasy meat and stuffed it into their faces, wiping their hands on their furry tunics. The men ate like starving wolves, never noticing their hostess as she cringed at the head of the table.

King Irv *did* notice his lady's displeasure, but what could he do? It wasn't his job to teach these strange sailors table manners. His queen leaned close to his ear to whisper, "Are you sure these men are from the *future*? They seem very primitive to me."

Judith stepped up behind her mother. "The Romans who brought civilization to our island never got as far as the northern lands. These men are probably from about halfway between our age and the time where Rutherford, Tiffany and I live. I remember reading that in their place in history, they raid our English isles to plunder our treasures, rape our women and kill lots of people. I just hope it isn't *our* fault that they discovered England," she said glaring at Hershel with daggered eyes.

The Merlin tried to melt back into the woodwork.

"It isn't Hershel's fault," Rutherford put in. "When he died he probably just abandoned his time machine where he usually parked it. I'm just surprised that whatever it is that allows jumping around in time lasted some four or five hundred years. There must be some pretty strong magic involved here… Or science."

"Crystals are alive… They're living things," the Merlin wailed. "They might be able to live forever, for all I know."

"But the tin your contraption is made of?" King Irv questioned.

Before Hershel could come up with an answer, a man came through the door dressed in rags; a tattered old green wool sweater, shiny pants with worn-away knees and holes in the backside, with his feet were covered in falling apart leather boots. He didn't sport the animal skins the others in his troop wore.

"Aye, mate." He doffed the faded cloth cap from his head and bowed to King Irv. "I'm Miles. Thor's lieutenant said you speak me own English tongue and I should drop by and have a natter."

After Irv introduced his family to the man Queen Sophie stuttered," A,a,and you're one of these, these, a, Northmen?"

"Not really, love, urm, I mean your highness, just a simple fisherman. I got in a spot of bother off the coast with a strong gale. Me boat got swamped and me mates washed over the side and disappeared. As I was prayin' God would have mercy on my drowning soul, these chaps showed up in a big boat with a dragon's head at the front. The hauled me in, gave me some grub and water and put me in a hammock until I was feelin' a bit better.

"So I figured, as I had just cheated death, I might just be up for a spot of adventure and I signed on with the crew." Miles smiled a smug smile. King Irv handed the fisherman a tankard of strong ale and Thor nodded his head toward the rapidly diminishing platter of cold roast beef.

CHAPTER FIVE

The ale flowed freely through the afternoon. The Viking captain's English seemed to improve the more he spoke to King Irv's people and the more ale he imbibed. Thor's men were curious about everything. Princes Judith organized a tour for them, leading the Northmen up the road to what was originally her Roadside Attraction, and now the wine bar of Debbie Manischewitz. The Viking sailors were fascinated by Smokey, the wine bar's tame dragon. They drank glass after glass of Dragon's Blood wine, a cheap table red, while feeding scraps of their pizza to Smokey as he danced behind his barrier.

Debbie kept cautioning the men that pizza wasn't good for the dragon, which was normally fed stray sheep and goats, but the laughing Vikings continued without paying her any mind.

"Better scraps of this interesting new food than the members of my crew," one of the Viking sailors quipped.

While the crewmen were touring Wholesale kingdom, Thor and his English cohort, Miles, accompanied Hershel to his cave. Irv's ginger maugy, Bird, stuck close to the Viking captain, seemingly infatuated with the red-bearded stranger. As Hershel attempted to explain his scientific studies, a discussion erupted between Miles and Thor.

Thor stated his belief that they could sail far to the west and find new lands. "A sailor named Leif Erickson has been to some of these new lands," he declared.

"Just jolly lucky he didn't sail right off the edge of the world," Miles scoffed. "Me mates and I were jolly close to the rim when the water swamped our little ketch. I'm pretty sure the world is as flat as a dinner plate."

Hershel the Merlin was chuckling in the background. "Gentlemen," he laughed, "Do you want to see what the world really looks like? I have a proven model right here if you're interested." At this point, Hershel brought forth the future globe Rutherford had given him.

"You see here a true map of our world, as round as an egg."

"Oh please," Miles protested, "I don't think this ball thing will pass muster with the True Church."

"And you trust this church as the ultimate answer?" King Irv asked. "Because I have been halfway around this world, to a place called San Francisco on the far side of this globe... And I didn't fall off. I wasn't even shaken."

While Miles cringed back into the cave walls as though lightning would strike him at any moment, Thor smiled and nodded. "I've always believed something similar," he smiled. "So many captains have reported such things to me."

Thor then borrowed a large sheep skin that Hershel had hanging to cure near the entrance to his cave and a small piece of charcoal. The Viking chief proceeded to draw a crude map of the North Atlantic based on what he saw on Hershel's globe.

"I'd like to set out and find this big land to the west," he told his hosts. "Erickson and his crew spoke well of it. They called it Vinland because wild wine grapes grew there in abundance. Personally, I much prefer ale to wine, but that's beside the point."

At this point in the discussion, Princess Judith shimmered in the cave door, remaining very quiet and unobtrusive.

"Vinland sounds about right," Hershel chuckled. "I been there a few times, just north of this San Francisco place, and the land is loaded with good grapes. I even brought some back to make wine for her highness, Queen Sophie. But they brew some excellent ale there as well. King Irv's son-in-law owns a brewery in that San Francisco city.

"And what a wild city that is," Hershel continued, "Scantily clad ladies sunning themselves on the beaches and motor cars everywhere."

"Motor cars?" Thor inquired, "Never heard such an English word before. What exactly is a motor car?"

Thor then noticed Princess Judith and glanced her way to see if she had an explanation or translation for him. She did not.

Hershel rolled his eyes. "Uh, kinda like a cart that moves on its own without any horse attached?"

"The devil's magic," whispered Miles, crossing himself. "I don't want any part of a place like that!" The Englishman then proceeded to down his entire mug of strong ale and held it out for a refill to calm his Christian nerves.

Thor and King Irv grinned at each other as though sharing an interesting joke. "There's such a thing as progress," Thor told the English sailor. "An open mind will always find new ideas to ponder and new truths to shape his world. This globe thing of Hershel's is such an advancement. The man says he's been to this new world across the seas on more than one occasion and has met and talked to people there. I am inclined to believe him, the church be damned."

Miles crossed himself again and glanced skyward, waiting for lightning to strike down on these blasphemers, but nothing happened.

Princess Judith broke the tension. "I brought some pizzas down for you guys since you didn't take the tour with Thor's men. Who wants pizza with meat and who prefers pizza with river fish topping?"

CHAPTER SIX

Queen Sophie's party had taken place the night before, and had been a big success, but a party was always in order, so King Irv announced a second night of celebration in honor of his new buddies from the great lands of the north.

King Irv sent a handful of his own knights to guard the anchored Viking ship so that all Thor's men would be able to attend the feast. Hershel was there to give all the assigned knights of Wholesale strict instructions not to touch his time travel box which was attached to the Viking ship's mast, although he knew that Irv's loyal soldiers would never do such a thing. Bird the cat rolled his eyes in Irv's direction. Just how far could one trust humans.

As he trudged back to Warehouse Castle from the shore of the North Sea, Hershel was deep in thought about his invention. From all he understood about time and space, he couldn't figure out how his time travel device could be in two places in the universe at once. Especially two places in the same exact *time*. Was it the power of the crystals? Or was it just how the universe was structured?

No matter, somehow his clever invention existed across the time it accessed, far beyond its humble beginnings. Was there a way he could ever control this gap in the universe or had he opened a giant temporal Pandora's Box across space?

As quickly as the Merlin arrived home, he poured himself a giant litre mug of ale, finished it in four swallows and poured himself another. He rapidly shook his head to clear his thoughts then finished his second ale. He looked down to find King Irv's ginger maugy on his lap wearing a sort of Cheshire grin. Hershel contemplated a third mug, but decided he'd had enough. It was time to gather his wits about himself and go to speak with King Irv. He stroked Bird's soft fur for another moment, then pushed the cat from his lap, preparing to rise.

His monarch saved him the trouble, stumbling across the first fairway down the path from the castle to the Merlin's cave.

"You're the man of science," King Irv told his magician. "I may be your king, but most of my learning comes from studying the Torah and observing life as a prince when my father occupied the throne of Wholesale. Before my time we never had public education, besides Torah study, for the young men of the synagogue." When the King had taken a seat, Bird leaped into his lap.

"I hear what you're sayin', highness," Merlin replied, with a thoughtful pose, "But I never went to any real school either. Remember, highness, I'm a couple years older then you.

"I was taught about the history of our small tribe by Mel of the Brooks, the old man who used to live in that falling-down windmill where the sixth fairway is now. Besides being a really funny guy, Old Mel could recite everything important that ever happened to our people as far back as when Old Levi snuck his family out of Israel and landed on the southern shores of Rome. By the way, Irv, excuse my bad manners. Could I offer you a wee dram of ale?"

"I thought you'd never ask," Irv chuckled, stroking the ginger tabby in his lap. "So, how old would Old Mel be if he was still with us? Probably close to one-hundred…"

"He was one-hundred when he passed," Hershel barked, "And what was that, almost fifteen years ago?" Bird turned to his king with a scolding look.

King Irv took a deep draught from the mug Hershel handed him, wiped the foam from his lips with the back of his hand and, with a faraway look commented, "How time flies..."

The pair sat in silence for some time, savoring Hershel's home-brewed strong ale, when there was a rustling outside the cave's entrance.

"Thor thought we might find you here," came the voice of the English fisherman from the future, Miles. "Can we join you? Thor has some questions to ask about the world, your Gods, and life in general."

"By all means, come in," Irv called. "Hershel, can we have some ale for our visitors?" Bird the cat quickly jumped from Irv's lap to that of the Viking chieftain, Thor.

When they all had mugs in front of them, Miles began, "We've heard that your time machine is somewhat limited in the number of people it can carry." Hershel only nodded at this statement while Thor tugged at his fellow sailor's sleeve and poured out a torrent of Norwegian to the man.

Miles continued, "We understand that your family wishes to return to their homes in the future and that they fear they must be separated and taken back one at a time, even the little girl."

Irv turned his head to stare at Hershel. Hershel shrugged his shoulders and turned to his king. "I never said anything, highness." They both swiveled their heads back to stare at Thor.

In his halting English, sporting a wide grin, Thor declared, "We take everyone back to their time at once. Long boat holds many people. In exchange, you show how to make jumps in time. Show how to work knob on crystal's box."

CHAPTER SEVEN

After another round of drinks, Irv and Hershel returned to Warehouse Castle with Thor and Miles. Irv hadn't given a definite answer, yeah or nay, about Thor's men taking his family back to the future, but it was a thought worth considering. The king's cat, Bird, followed close on the heels of the Viking leader, purring loudly and clearly smitten with this hairy stranger.

Hershel had, at the start of Queen Sophie's party, complained about the stress of so much time travel. And a ride in a Viking ship could prove an exciting adventure for his family. Irv knew that his son-in-law, Rutherford, with his fascination about history, would probably love the idea.

Of course King Irv had no concept of how the sight of Viking marauders in 2016 England would affect the people of that time. Strange men crossing his golf course in his own time hadn't seemed that frightening an event, but then he understood that some time in between, Viking sailors had raped, looted and pillaged this island they all lived on. Were the people from Rutherford's time still terrified by these wild Vikings? He would have to consult Rabbi Weiss before he could make such a commitment.

Irv found the good Rabbi in his study, pouring over the ancient Torah scrolls. King Irv knocked on the side of his door, just above the mezuzah. "Teacher?" the king called, "Have you got a minute?"

"Oy," the old man answered without looking up from his study, "Have I got a minute? I've got a *lifetime*, so how can I help you already?"

"Ah, what do you know of Viking people, teacher?" Irv inquired.

"Viking people? What the hell are Viking people? I've never encountered such a thing in the Torah." The Rabbi leaned back and set his scroll down on his desk. "So tell me about Viking people."

"Well," Irv hesitated, "We've just had a boatload of them land on our shore. They have bright red hair and beards and they claim to come from some land far to the north. They appear to be unkempt and primitive, but they seem quite intelligent.

"And they're partying like madmen right now up at my castle."

"Could these people be another of our lost tribes of Israel?" the Rabbi inquired. "Do they speak Hebrew?"

"Ah, teacher, don't you remember?" Irv reminded the man of God, "You were playing golf with us when these guys showed up out of the woods. You tried some Hebrew on them and it went right over their heads."

"Och, *those* Vikings," the Rabbi coughed. "Yes, I remember now... No, I can't help you with these people. They're not from Canaan or Jericho, are they?"

"I don't think so," the monarch answered. "They claim to be from someplace they call Norway, where it gets very cold and sometimes the sun never sets, and other times it's night for most of the day."

The Rabbi picked up his Torah scroll and began rolling it open again. "Well," he smiled, "It would seem that you know much more about these people then I do." Then he dismissively pushed his nose into the Torah. King Irv showed himself out.

With no guidance from his Rabbi, King Irv decided to turn to his son, Prince Sol. He found the prince in the main hall of Vaud Castle in the neighboring kingdom, very squiffy, arm wrestling one of Thor's men on a table in the main hall. Bird the cat sat purring on the table just out of reach. Whose side the tomcat was rooting for, King Irv couldn't tell.

"Ah, son," the monarch inquired, "Have you got a moment?"

"Anything for you, Pops," Prince Sol replied. "By the way, you care to bet a few shekels on me before I take this brute down? I know I've got him beat from the get-go."

Before Irv could make his case to his son, he felt a heavy arm lowered across his back. He turned his head to meet the bloodshot and very drunk eyes of Thor.

"You are good king," the Viking chieftain praised, patting Irv's shoulder, "You are not, how you say, bamboozled, by these Christian people, like my King Olaf was. I proud to have you as friend. I love Wholesale Kingdom, and Vaud Kingdom as well." He then shouted, "Someone give King Irv more ale. We drink a toast to friendship between our peoples."

With no one left to counsel him, King Irv finally relented and agreed that Thor should bring his family back to England in the 2000s, but he made it clear that he and Hershel would go along to see that everything went right and his family would return to the right time and place, and safely. Bird the Cat winked at him. He wanted to go along as well.

CHAPTER EIGHT

The Northmen remained in Wholesale for the rest of the week. Some of King Irv's knights helped the Norwegian sailors caulk loose boards in their ship's hull while others filled empty barrels with fresh water and ale. The Viking sailors were used to salt pork, but as that wasn't kosher, Irv's men brought them stores of cold, salted beef for their larder. By the Sabbath, the longboat was ready to sail but Irv persuaded them to wait until the high tide after Saturday sundown before they weighed anchor. They should all respect the Sabbath.

Princess Judith and Tiffany were provided a special tent on the middle deck for their short passage across the ages. Rutherford and Irving stood at the stearboard rail beside Thor's crew. Hershel crouched at the base of the ship's lone mast with one of Thor's lieutenants named Lars to operate the time travel device.

Bird the cat had somehow snuck aboard. The ginger tabby divided his time between his king and his new Norwegian best friend.

At a sign from Thor, Lars looked to Hershel for assurance, and when the Merlin nodded, he turned the dial ever so slightly then pressed it in.

Everyone on board held tightly to ropes or rails as the longboat began to vibrate. The next thing they knew, they were parked in a narrow stream of water with lush green trees on either bank and fields to match beyond the stream. Bicycles whizzed by on the footpath near the river and picnickers stared open mouthed at them.

Thor and his men seemed in a sudden panic. No one could understand what was going on. Rutherford walked to the ship's prow and looked forward, recognizing a crowded footbridge across the Thames River less than a quarter mile ahead of them.

"Break out the oars," he shouted, "Full ahead!"

Less than half the crew responded to this dark-skinned foreigner, but their paddling was enough to send the boat forward under the narrow footbridge. As the dragon's head on the nose of Thor's ship slipped under the wooden structure, Rutherford gathered his wife and daughter, boosting them up onto the wooden planks and then himself leaping into the river water, just short of the bank.

Those manning the oars had to commence a rapid back paddle to reverse the long boat before it might take out the bridge with its tall mast. Their vessel came to a halt with their sail just four feet from the rails of the Thames Bridge, raising panic among Vikings and shore bound Englishmen as well.

King Irv found himself cheated of the opportunity to say goodbye to his family, but at the same time, he noticed uniformed officers emerging from motor cars with blue lights flashing on their tops. The police activity all seemed to be focused on the Viking ship on which he was riding.

King Irv blew a kiss to his daughter and granddaughter, shouted his goodbyes and then turning to Hershel, he shouted, "Better get us out of here, and as quickly as you can."

Rutherford, the princess and Tiffany quickly caught a taxi up the river toward their home in Oxford. Hershel's settings had brought them as far up the Thames as was navigable by a boat such as Thor's. When Irv's family reached the safety of a pub near their dwelling, they listened to wild rumors about some ecology group who had built an old Viking style longboat and had staged a protest where the Thames met the River Coln. Already crowds of young people had been gathering, but King Irv or Thor could have known nothing of this... Or could they? Rutherford always wondered just how psychically connected these old time Jews might be.

As their cab made its way north toward Oxford University housing, Judith and her family could see the carloads of Thames Valley Police headed in the opposite direction, towards where Thor and his men had left them off.

Meanwhile, back at Inglesham, near the junction of the rivers Thames and Coln, police and civilians alike stared at the ancient ship as it shimmered for a few seconds and then disappeared, briefly leaving the impression of its hull in the calm waters. Oxford students with the ecology protest cheered while Thames River Valley constables shouted, gnashed their teeth and pulled at their hair.

"It was a fair cop," shouted one senior detective on the anti-terrorism squad. "So what are these buggers playing at? And how could they make something that big simply vanish?"

"Probably an illusion," his sergeant nodded. "You know, done with them laser things... Like a hologram."

Part II
The Northmen Take Over

CHAPTER NINE

Thor's lieutenant, Lars, had already studied Hershel's globe and memorized the coordinates for the eastern coast of Vinland, where he believed they should go. As the modern police accosted their ship, these were the numbers he dialed into the Merlin's time travel device when the magician wasn't looking.

So, when Thor's vessel disappeared from the river Thames, it materialized in what would later be known as Narragansett Bay, north of the Rhode Island Sound. And as luck would have it, there were other Viking sailors standing on the shore to their east to greet them. On a hill overlooking the bay was a tall tower of stone, similar to church towers Thor and his men had seen at the entrance to the Baltic, on the island of Bornholm.

"Are you sure we've reached a time before Leif landed?" Thor questioned aloud.

Hershel bent down to examine the dials of his captured device. "Eh, nice try, Ace," he aimed sarcastically at Lars, who was now cringing under Thor's own stare. "I think you found the place you wanted, but your time setting was off by a hundred years or so."

Lars stood up, red faced, and shrugged. His look said, "How was I to know, this is all new to me."

King Irv fumed and paced the deck. "I thought you'd be taking us directly home?" he barked at the Viking captain.

"Well, we're here now," Thor announced, avoiding the Wholesale monarch's question, "Might as well make the most of it." He smiled as he directed his men to row toward an open docking space along the bay's edge. Irv's ginger tabby, Bird, grinned down mockingly at Lars from the Viking chieftain's shoulder. When King Irv glared at his host, Bird climbed into the rigging and sat back to lick his private parts.

"Wait a minute," King Irv thundered from the boat's prow, "I ask you again, what about taking us back to Wholesale Kingdom? I thought we had an understanding here."

Thor turned to Irv with a sheepish grin. "Well," he schmoozed, "We were hoping you could stay with us for a short while longer, until we got the hang of this time travel thing. After all, you and your friend *are* the experts in this."

"That's not what we agreed to," Irv sneered, his right foot pounding a nervous rhythm on the planking of the ship's deck. He stared at his pal, Bird, thinking that the ginger tabby had somehow betrayed him.

Thor shrugged. "So, do you want to leave our company here? If you do, I don't know how to help you get home."

"You can jolly well readjust that time travel set and take us home right now!" Irv thundered. "When we're back near my castle in our own time, Hershel can set the dial correctly for you so you can arrive before this Leif guy or all these Danes."

Hershel knelt down to adjust the dial to take them home, but found a half dozen broad swords surrounding him, aimed at his thin frame.

"Well," Lars interjected with a nod towards his men, "Hershel did agree to spend the time to familiarize us with his, uh, time travel thingy's controls."

"And that's just what you'll be doing for a week or two here, highness," Thor chuckled. "When my men have this time thing under control, we'll gladly ferry you home to your time. Maybe we can tarry there for a short while and you can teach us this golf game of yours."

King Irv uttered a curse under his breath, then turned a smile to his erstwhile captors. "We will go along with this for now... But mark my words... my kingdom will *not* be pleased with your attitude. We will not want you to learn about golf, or any other of our amusements. At some point, we may even wish to exact some payment from you and your own kingdom."

Meanwhile, Thor's crew rowed them alongside the wharf of a community the Danish Jom Vikings called 'Høp.' A captain calling himself Hansen came forward to welcome them. He cocked his head and listened for a minute, then called out, "Norsemen? I thought you'd all left for the south to find your own special land?"

Thor quickly translated and then looked at King Irv, but the Jewish monarch didn't have a clue. If only Rutherford were here with them he might have some inkling from the history he had studied. Vinland appeared to be such a large place, its coast longer than the whole of the island that contained the Wholesale Kingdom. How could anyone be found along such a long stretch of ocean?

Hansen offered them a place to come ashore, camp and organize their further expedition. "We've all come to this new land as brothers," Hansen told them. "There is so much room here for all our tribes to prosper. And the Scralings, the native people, have become friendly after we began trading our red wool cloth with them. Of course, they want to trade things for our swords as well, but I don't think that such a good idea." Hansen gave a nervous laugh.

"Some of my men have taken wives from the local Scraling folk, which has helped us to bond with them. Some of these native folks have even accepted the new Christian ideas a few of our men expound…"

"I don't care for these new Christian ideas!" Thor interrupted and spit in the grass by his side, at which Hansen laughed louder.

"I'm not keen on these crazy ideas myself," he told Thor. Miles quickly translated for King Irv and Hershel.

"We've already had some Italian man here, claiming to represent the True Church. Called himself the Bishop of Greenland or some such thing, we sent him packing."

Fidgeting in the background, Hershel the Merlin finally asked, "So can we get a drink here? My mouth is so dry I'm spitting Spanish peat."

Miles translated with a chuckle and Hansen apologized profusely, turning to shout at some of his men along the quayside. "Ale for our Norseman guests!" Hansen called out, then turning back to Thor and Irv, he said, "Ale is on the way. Our brewing operations are not what we'd like them to be, this new land being so different from the European coast, but we do have some fairly good brew to offer for hospitality."

Miles translated with a grin and the small entourage followed the Danish captain to a large hall just up the hill, toward the old Viking church tower.

CHAPTER TEN

Irv and Hershel were very unhappy with their current situation, but Thor had posted a heavy guard around the ship's mast, where the time contraption was affixed. Thor and Lars, enjoying their drink of ale and swapping stories with the Danes late into the nights on shore, didn't seem to be in any hurry to set sail any time soon.

Finally, after almost a week, King Irv put his foot down. Approaching a rather squiffy Thor as he returned to the ship in the early morning hours from the Danish captain's hall, he told the Viking chief that Hershel had some very powerful magic, magic which could bring grave misfortune on their ship if they didn't get on with their business.

"Mark my words," Irv bellowed, "you could stand to lose your ship and many of your men if Hershel is forced to summon his powerful storm your way. It will be a storm of powerful, swirling winds and torrential rain like you have never experienced before. It will come to you without warning, so you should be constantly looking over your shoulder... That is, if you don't keep your promise to bring us home to our own land and time."

Sailors, being a suspicious lot, were easily frightened at the mention of either storms or magic. Thor was already in awe of Hershel's power in that he could come up with something like a time machine to begin with.

Sick and hung-over, Thor and Lars gathered their crew and weighed anchor at first light. They sailed southwest, hugging the coastline, skirting both Cape Cod and Long Island and keeping their lookouts alert for other Viking ships, or anyone else, in the area. Among themselves, they discussed if Hershel the Merlin might have the power to bring forth such a storm. In the end, they decided to press on. If this Englishman had such a power, they would wait to find out.

As they passed the entrance to New York Harbor, King Irv asked Lars how this sailing south was helping them to learn anything about Hershel's time machine. "I thought that learning about this thing was the reason we're still on board and traveling with you."

But the Vikings could give him no good answer. Bird glared down at his King from Thor's shoulder. "We'll let you know when we reach a good spot where we may tarry and learn about all this," Thor told them, "I don't think it would be well to learn about such things in an open ocean. Then the Viking Chieftain ordered his men to make a quick turn, eighty-five degrees to stearboard and up the Hudson River.

It turned out to be almost a three day excursion. The Vikings were curious about every bend in the wide stream. They halted to explore the Jersey palisades and, on their return towards the sea, they dropped anchor and sent a small party to explore the future island of Manhattan. On this lush, fertile island, they met more Scralings, American natives, with whom they traded goat cheese and wool cloth for fresh vegetables and grapes. The natives also threw in a couple pipes and some broad green leaves that the Viking sailors could pack into pipes and smoke. These tobacco leaves that Thor's sailors smoked made most of them nauseous and as quickly as they put back out to sea, they tossed the pipes over the side, with the exception of one or two men who claimed that these tobacco leaves gave them great strength and clarity of though.

King Irv and Hershel had both thought that the sheltered waters of the Hudson River would be a perfect place to hold a few lessons in dealing with the time travel device, but every time they approached either Thor or Lars, the senior Vikings were too busy scanning the shoreline on either side of their vessel for any sign that some other crew had proceeded them here.

Leaving New York harbor, the long boat passed a quiet night at sea, awaking to the dawn somewhere off the coast of future New Jersey. Still no word of training in the art of time travel. The seas were calm. The ship almost sailed itself, leaving some of the crewmen bored and restless. Thor scanned the coast, watchful for anything of interest, but found nothing remarkable.

Just before mid day, two of the younger Viking sailors started playing at mock sword battles to pass the time. They jumped about, from the deck to the outer rails, into the rigging and around the ship's lone mast. After a leap from the stearboard railing, one of the young sailors, named Burr, missed the ropes holding up the mast and landed flat out on the deck. As he fell, his sword flew forward from his hand and into Hershel's time machine, knocking off the main control dial and sending forth a puff of smoke from the small box containing the mechanism. Irv's maugy, Bird, arched his back in the rigging and gave a deep, morbid growl.

King Irv and Hershel were on the forward deck at the time, arguing again with Lars that they should finish training the Vikings on how to use the time travel thingy so they could be taken home. This delaying had gone far enough. King Irv had important matters to attend to back in the Wholesale Kingdom. The cry of the fallen sailor and the howl from Bird brought their attention around to the ship's tall mast, where small wisps of smoke continued to emanate from the diminutive time travel cube.

Hershel slapped his forehead. "Oy vey," he shouted. "What have you done…? And who has done it?" Hershel and his monarch quickly beat feet for the center of the boat.

Burr remained slightly dazed, lying face down on the wooden deck. His adversary in the mock battle had disappeared to somewhere in the ship's rear quarter, possibly putting himself into a seat by the ship's outer rail, to pretend to be one of the duty oarsmen.

Thor followed, hot on the heels of both king and Merlin, tearing at his bright red beard. "Ack," he cried, "Burr, what have you done? If you've hurt this thing which can take us through time…" Then, turning to Hershel, Thor chuckled, "Well, you made this thing. I'm sure you'll be able to sort it out and get it working again."

CHAPTER ELEVEN

Hershel knelt and gave his time machine a quick going over. The knob that he usually adjusted to set a distance in time and space had been sheared off just inside the box. Had the young sailor's sword penetrated beyond the surface? From where he was looking, Hershel couldn't tell, but he suspected something inside the box had been badly damaged. Oh, if only he had his small bag of tools with him to open the casing and look inside, fixing the time travel box would be a piece of cake.

Thor's ship continued its cruise down the coast of what would someday be called America. Beyond the Jersey Shore they stumbled into Delaware Bay and Thor insisted that it would be worth a day or two of exploring. In his mind, Thor was still suspicious that some other Viking crew might have preceded them. He had to know if there were any other settlements in this or any other inlet, like the Danes he'd encountered when they'd first arrived through time.

Delaware Bay took less time to explore then the Hudson River, and by the next day, they were back on their southern course along the Vinland Coast. They had sailed for another disinteresting handful of days when a lookout spotted another large inlet just around the end of what would later be known as Cape Charles.

It was a Sunday and the Vikings had now been at sea for a fortnight since leaving the Danish colony of Høp. It took them another full week to sail up the Chesapeake Bay and back. Thor's ship was about to re-enter the Atlantic Ocean, when one of Thor's men pointed out another watery avenue, and the long boat made a right turn into the mouth of the James River.

By now, King Irv was tearing at his hair. His best friend, Bird the cat, was still infatuated with the crazy Viking captain and Hershel wasn't making any progress with his broken time machine. There was little to do besides drink endless tankards of ale and watch the unspoiled shores of Vinland roll by.

CHAPTER TWELVE

They took a detour up the James River into future Virginia, where they spent a couple nights in the company of other Norwegian Vikings who had settled on the banks of that broad stream. At this small colony, they met a baby, Snorri, the first Viking child born in the new world, according to the child's proud parents. This hearty lot told a tale of how they had stopped an attack by hostile Scralings. The natives had become frightened when a bull from the Viking encampment had escaped and charged at them. To retaliate, they attacked the Vikings, twirling hornet's nests from long poles and then hurling them in the Northmen's direction. Many of the Viking sailors had retreated in terror, but one brave Viking woman, Snorri's mother, stood against them. She dropped her top and slapped a sword to her ample bare breast with a loud war whoop. The natives were so terrified of a woman who would challenge them that they immediately retreated and the battle was won.

King Irv was anxious to know how Viking women had come to Vinland. "Some of our explorers came with the assumption that they would find free new land to settle," Thor told him. "That was the second wave of explorers to this new world."

"But you have no women aboard your ship," the English monarch observed. "What is the reason for this?"

"Because I have not come so much to settle as to have my name repeated throughout history as the man who discovered this new world."

"But you did no such thing," Hershel exclaimed. "You're about a hundred years too late."

Thor chuckled. "That is why your time travel machine is so crucial to me and my men. Once we've established who and when were the first Vikings to land here, your machine can bring us to this new land months, days, or even just hours before they land. These explorers will find *me* on the beach, and I will be the one honored in the sagas of discovery. I will be the man remembered in history forever after."

"But sir," Hershel exclaimed, "I've been to the future, I mean the far off future, and they don't honor any Viking. The people in the distant future celebrate some Italian named Columbus. They even have a bank holiday in America in his name: Columbus Day."

"I refuse to believe this," Thor thundered emphatically. "It must be Thor's Day that they celebrate after I best Leif Ericson with the help of your time thingy."

"Suit yourself," Hershel tossed off with a skeptical look. "But that ain't what Rutherford told us."

⚜ CHAPTER THIRTEEN ⚜

L eaving the Viking colony on the James River, the longboat continued its drift down the long seacoast of this new land. Through it all, Hershel continued to probe the depths of his time travel box through the tiny hole left by the missing knob.

After two more day of drifting along narrow barrier islands, the Vikings put in once more to a wide and sheltered bay. They spent a day or so rowing north behind the skinny, sandy islands, then drifted south once more along the coast to the west where they came upon more rivers heading into this wild new land.

Sailing up another of these streams, in what would someday be called North Carolina, Thor and his men encountered more natives. They stopped to trade some of their wool cloth for fresh green vegetables, and as they did, King Irv cocked his head and listened. After tuning in to the natives conversing among themselves, he strolled forward down the ship's gang plank to greet these Vinland people. Thor's men were trying hand gestures and miming to establish communication with these natives.

Irv stepped into the group of Vikings and Vinlanders. "Shalom," he spoke loudly, to which one of the natives replied "Shalom" back to him with an unconcerned nod.

King Irv beckoned Hershel to join him and soon the two of them were conversing with these Vinland people in the old Hebrew tongue. Thor and his men stepped back aghast as the new conversation proceeded.

The leader of the so-called native group told Irv and Hershel a tale of ancestors sailing across the seas from what was thought to be the Holy Land after Roman soldiers tried to enslave his people. "The Egyptians did it once, we weren't about to be taken in again," he told Irv and Hershel. The Vikings watched from the sidelines.

"Some of our people," the tribal elder told Irv, "went to Rome to start a new life, but we were fearful of these Roman soldiers, so we kept sailing west."

"Interesting," King Irv told the native man. "My people tried to settle in Rome after leaving Israel. We lived there for a generation, but we weren't happy. Our young generation set sail for a new Roman colony on an island to the west. I've learned from other settlers that our island was called England."

"But this England place," his new friend asked, "was it not also ruled by Roman soldiers?"

"For a short while, yes," Irv told the man, "but eventually they returned home as their empire was collapsing. We were able to establish our own small Jewish kingdom there, the Wholesale Kingdom."

"And we're doing very well, thank you," Hershel chimed in with a grin.

"And *we* are doing well here," their host told them. "By the way, I'm Abe Cher. We call my people Cherokee. Most of us have settled here on this fertile coast, but some of the young families from our tribe have ventured west to open new lands."

"And I'm King Irving David," Irv told them, extending his hand. "This is my man of magic, Hershel," he went on with a tip of his head to the Merlin.

"Our pleasure to make your acquaintance," Abe Cher told them.

From the sidelines, Thor's lieutenant Lars called out in a loud whisper. "See if they have any greens to trade."

Hershel tipped his head in acknowledgement of the request and asked Abe Cher the question.

"Trade?" the native man bellowed. "It is an honor to meet fellow Jews. We will be happy to share our abundance of the crops we've grown from this new soil. Just tell us what you might require."

Later that day, a feast was organized. Thor's crew was fed venison along with a variety of salad greens, but the hit of the day was a small red thing the Cherokee's boiled for them called a potato. No one mentioned that Thor and his crew were not Jewish.

After the dinner, Abe Cher brought forth animal bladders filled with a potent red wine to share with Irv and Hershel. The two Englishmen stayed up most of the night swapping stories with the Cherokee people. The Norsemen kept to themselves, drinking the proffered wine. They had nothing to say to these Scralings who spoke King Irv's tongue.

Before they weighed anchor the next day, the Norse sailors filled their hold with small, red potatoes as King Irv and Hershel bid their long lost brethren farewell. "We'll keep an eye out for your pioneer families as we explore the west," Hershel told Abe Cher. "Maybe one day we'll get back this way to see you again."

"Mahzel," Abe Cher called after them. "Go with God."

CHAPTER FOURTEEN

As they sailed on south from the Cherokee colony, Hershel and his king noticed the days getting hotter and more humid, but Hershel kept on at his work, drinking ever more ale to cope with the humidity. He was vaguely aware of the boat making intermittent stops along the way, where they would briefly go ashore to check out the land. He'd long since lost track of the days. It seemed like they'd been drifting along this new world for months.

Lars, Thor's second in command, said they had heard rumors of an Irish settlement somewhere on this coast. Thor was obsessed with finding this Irishman, Brendan the Bold, to pick his brains about this vast new continent.

Summer was approaching, the sun high in the sky, when they steered the boat into the mouth of a wide river in a humid tropical land, and a party of Vikings went ashore. They soon came back with a report that Burr had been consumed by a dragon.

"A dragon?" King Irv queried, "A fire breathing dragon?"

"Don't know about fire," one of the young Norwegian marines told him through Mile's interpretation, with his eyes firmly focused on his shoes, "but it were definitely a dragon, sir."

"And did it have wings?" King Irv asked, "Two sets of large wings?"

Miles, the Englishman, conferred back and forth with the man before replying.

"Didn't see any wings," Miles told him the man had replied, shuffling rapidly from foot to foot, "but he's sure it was a dragon, sir."

"Describe this 'dragon,' if you can," Hershel put in. "I've known a few dragons and I can tell you that if it's the real George, I'll recognize it."

More dialogue passed between Miles and the young Viking. The sailor continued to shift his weight from one foot to the other. "It was a noxious green in color, and very scaly." Miles reported. "When it opened its mouth, the thing's breath was quite foul. The wind from the thing's mouth could certainly burn like fire! It flew forward from the water on the devil's wings, grabbed Burr, and dragged him down into the river. It was horrible to watch! Burr fought for his life, but the dragon had a firm hold on him and dragged poor Burr down under the water's surface."

The youthful sailor nodded his agreement as Miles relayed his story.

"But it didn't *fly* on wings," King Irv persisted. "Did this monster spray fire from mouth?" he asked. "Was there smoke coming from its nostrils?"

"We didn't see any fire," another of the young sailors who knew some English confirmed, "though we felt a bit fevered watching it."

Bird the cat grinned like his namesake from County Cheshire.

King Irv had to laugh, "These are not dragons, they are but large lizards. Dragons are intelligent creatures, like Smokey back at my castle. These paltry lizards don't have any wings and probably possess very small brains. They're dangerous, to be sure. I'd give them a wide berth, if I were you... But they are *not* anything like real dragons."

Miles waved his arms about as he relayed King Irv's words back to the assembled crew.

As they prepared to depart this terrible coast, Thor forbid his sailors to leave the ship, to swim in the warm tropical waters, and especially to go ashore in this God forsaken land with lizards which consumed sailors for supper. But young Vikings were of a mind of their own. Adolescent men dived from the rails when no one was looking. They swam to the nearby Everglades where they fished and hunted small birds. One young Viking was carried away by a large dark cat while another fell victim to another of those large lizard creatures.

As quickly as the news of the fate of these sailors's returned with the miscreant crew members, Thor demanded that the long-boat put out to sea once more. Fearing these dragon-like lizards, Thor gave this portion of the new land a wide berth, sailing west around what appeared to be the land's end of Vinland and then north through hundreds of small islands. They continued on, hugging the coast until the sea appeared more open. In the lee of this large, wild land, Thor dropped his anchor off some new barrier islands, probably near future Sarasota, Florida.

"This would be a good place to test your time thingy," he announced to Hershel and the Merlin's king.

"Oh yeah, right," Hershel exploded. "One of your men, who they say was eaten by a large lizard, stuck a sword into my time machine. Unless you've got the right tools to help me fix it, there ain't no time machine to learn about!"

"I'm so sorry," Thor demurred. "No one told me of this."

King Irv and Hershel exchanged looks. Could this be so? Hadn't they discussed this problem with the Viking chieftain months before? Well, true or false, it was immaterial at this point. They were stuck here in the waters of time.

Thor decided that, much as he'd like to learn about time travel, they might as well press onward until Hershel could restore the magic properties of his device. He had new lands to discover, lands that his people back in Norway might settle and prosper upon. And he, Thor, might someday be remembered as the man who opened the vast expanse of Vinland to the Norwegian people. That, in itself, was worth all the hardship that his men were enduring.

CHAPTER FIFTEEN

Weeks later, as they sat anchored in what would someday be called the Mississippi Delta, just off future New Orleans, Hershel again tried to fix his machine but to no avail. Thor and his men showed no sympathy. They seemed to be quite happy to simply explore the wilderness before them. Why worry about time travel when there was so much to see right before their very eyes in the here-and-now? And wasn't this their original objective, to further explore Vinland before other Viking captains could beat them to it? Wasn't that the attraction of the time travel thingy in the first place?

At the next dawn, Thor ordered his oarsmen to take them up this wide, swift river to the north and into the interior of this new land. There was so much land that could easily support the Norwegian families displaced by his homeland's overpopulation.

Thor's longboat headed north up this broad, muddy river, sometimes by the wind in their sails, but more often by the power of his broad-backed oarsmen. Thor's sailors observed more of these large lizards that they thought were dragons along the river's bank. They also saw villages of the local Scralings, who appeared to dominate the shores of Vinland.

After days of fighting the strong current this ribbon of water produced, Thor decided to beach his craft on the western shore of the great river, where another stream poured into it. The Northmen spent the night on the river's broad sandy bank. At daybreak, the Viking chieftain summoned his top men to a pow-wow on deck, in the shadow of the mast, where he organized two shore parties to march west across this new land and report back on the fertility of the land and the abundance of water and cattle feed. Thor put his friend, Lars, in command of the expedition and wished them the speed of all the Gods.

The remaining ship's crew waited. They filled their days with hunting the strange beasts of this new land, and fishing both the wide river and the stream that fed it. By night, they drank the last of the boat's ale while they played card games and threw dice. Two of Thor's lieutenant's harvested wild wheat from a few miles inland and began brewing fresh barrels of ale using old yeast from the ship's stores.

King Irv and his Merlin tore at their hair once more. Would they ever see their beloved England again? Hershel wavered between pondering solutions and fooling with the time box strapped to the ship's mast. King Irv was granted an audience with Thor almost daily, but the Viking captain continued to stall, promising that they would bring Irv and Hershel home as soon as he had finished his current explorations.

Just beyond another fortnight, the party of Vikings who had marched westward returned. They appeared to be well fed and thriving, and brought with them some kind of dried meat which they said gave them great energy.

All the ship's crew quickly gathered around the new arrivals to hear their tale, and the travelers didn't disappoint.

"Two days west, we met native Scralings who were most friendly," Lars reported. "They gave us this dried flesh from local beasts they called deer and antelope."

"This is excellent," Thor praised. "It is always good to be friends with the locals, just like our Danish brothers in Høp."

"They had no ale," Hans, one of the sailors, reported, "But they gave us small buttons from a plant, I think they called it a cactus. We chewed these buttons and suddenly we could see the gates of Valhalla! We were all flying with the Gods." Several of the Vikings from the exploration party began giggling at the thought.

Thor's brow creased in a frown. Getting silly with a tankard or two of ale he could understand, but cactus buttons that took men across the rainbow bridge to the gates of Valhalla without their earning a place there-in through hard work and battle? This was a bit worrying. How could men who'd already tasted Valhalla be disciplined and kept in line?

"And what else have you to report?" Thor asked in a skeptical tone. "Is there good grazing land for cattle? And abundant water?"

"There is, my captain," Lars called back to him, then hesitated for a long minute.

"And?" Thor prompted.

"Well," Lars gave back, staring at the toes of his boots, "there were also rune stones…"

"Rune stones?" Thor whispered back incredulously. "As in *Viking* rune stones?"

"It would seem so, captain," Lars replied, while his men all nodded their heads in the affirmative.

"So we are not the first even here…"

"I would venture to say that we are not, sir," Lars told him, eyes still fixed on the toes of his footwear.

"And did you see these rune stones before or after you chewed these strange buttons?" the captain smirked.

"Both," came his answer. "But before, with our wits clearly about us, we could read the message that someone else had been this way before us. These runes were clearly dated, 2 December 1022 on one stone and 24 November 1024 on the other."

"And their message?" Thor demanded.

"Urm, it was a bit unclear," Lars told him, finally lifting his eyes to meet his captain. "They seemed to be some variety of riddle that we could not solve."

CHAPTER SIXTEEN

News of the rune stones put Thor in a foul mood. He paced the deck much of the night, glaring at any man who might approach him. With the sunrise, he announced that they would float back down this river and, at its mouth, they would sail westward until they found a land where no Northman's foot had tread before them

"This new land has a lot to offer," Thor told himself, "But I would need to return with a small fleet of craft, along with a large group of men and women bent on settling here, to make it happen. And then, we must come to a place that no other Vikings can claim that they discovered first." He strongly believed that, when he made his report to the folks back home, he could assemble such a troop of pioneers.

Thor didn't confide his thoughts with his crew, especially not with King Irv or Hershel. His current crewmen were all fine fellows, but they were mostly young and adventurous. They weren't the type to take a bride, settle into a village, till a farm and raise good Norwegian families.

When he returned to Hardangerfjord, Thor would recruit only the top sailors, those with good backgrounds and families; people who could make Vinland a fine, exemplary land which could stand on its own.

Johan, one of the older sailors who was not so adventurous, had gone ashore, but spent his time combing the sandy banks for interesting stones and sea shells. On his return to the longboat, just before they turned around to float down the wide river, Johan couldn't wait to show off some of the treasures he'd collected. Most of his shipmates weren't interested in anything as tame as sea shells. Hershel, on the other hand, was fascinated by anything natural.

Hershel turned a shell over in his hand, feeling the texture and admiring the patterns of brown and beige. As he checked out the shell, he noticed that it was tapered at almost the same degree as one of the tools in his repair bag.

"Mind if I try something with your shell?" Hershel asked the seasoned Viking sailor.

"If it could be of some service to you," Johan replied.

Hershel inserted the narrow end of the shell into the gap in his time travel thingy where the knob had fallen off. He wiggled it around for a few seconds.

Part III
The Bayside Boogie

CHAPTER SEVENTEEN

Next thing they knew, the long boat began to shimmer. In a heartbeat, they found themselves sailing, not down a wide river in the wilderness, but under the Golden Gate Bridge into modern day San Francisco Bay.

Thor, frightened out of his mind by the large container ships and the tall buildings along the shoreline, maneuvered his small boat across the bay following Hershel's instructions and passed the old Alcatraz Island Prison and Yerba Buena Island to an open pier in a marina near Alameda.

King Irv looked around them to find that in the marina they were surrounded by sleek modern boats: sailing yachts, cabin cruisers and the occasional houseboat. The monarch nudged his man of magic.

"Ah, Hershel, do you remember when you first traveled to future England?" Hershel nodded, giving his king a questioning look.

"You did some kind of magic to make your time contraption blend in…"

Hershel shook his head up and down, thinking about what his king was telling him.

"So," King Irv whispered, "Look around you now. How many of these modern boats look anything like Thor's ancient vessel?"

Hershel did a quick three-sixty, then turned his eyes back to Irv. "Oy, you are so right, highness."

With a wink and a nod, Hershel conjured up a simple spell and Thor's old longboat suddenly appeared as a fifty-five foot yacht with smooth teak decks and rows of portholes along the gunwales where Viking shields had hung moments before. The Viking crew looked about them stunned, but Lars ordered them all below decks to the new luxury cabins. Plates of cheese and chocolate bars on the pillows of the new soft and wide beds entranced the Viking sailors, and they quickly fell under the Merlin's spell that put them to sleep, hopefully until they were ready to depart modern San Francisco.

Irv and Hershel bumped fists then turned to wink at Thor, who appeared thunderstruck. "Don't worry," Irv told the Viking chieftain, "Hershel knows what he's doing.

"I'm glad he does," the old Viking blinked, "Because I haven't got a clue what's going on." And at that, Irv, Thor and Hershel hot footed it down their gangplank and hailed a cab to the Metaphysical Brewing Company, owned by King Irv's son-in-law in the future, Rutherford, where they could secure some modern clothes and try to cover up their out-of-time situation. Hershel still didn't know how he could repair his time machine, but at least now he and his monarch held all the cards.

Luckily, King Irv still had his Barclay's Bank Master Card in one of the pockets of his royal robes, a card his son-in-law had given him for situations in future time just like this one. Bird the cat viewed their departure from the highest point on the boat's mast with feline skepticism, his tail waving rapidly to and fro.

"We're part of a Viking reenactment troop protesting Columbus Day," Irv told the edgy driver of the taxi who responded to their call.

"But Columbus Day isn't for another seven weeks," the credulous cabbie protested. At this, Hershel leaned forward in the back seat and told the man, "We're getting an early start, alright?"

"S, s, sure," the cabbie stuttered. He'd had all kinds of nut cases in his cab. After all, this *was* San Francisco. Older drivers had told him tales of ferrying Ken Kesey and Tim Leary from the university to various love-ins and be-ins. What was so strange about an early Columbus Day protest?

As it was a Wednesday morning, traffic was light across Oakland and Berkeley. They arrived at the Metaphysical Brewing Company in less than twenty minutes.

The taxi driver ran King Irv's Barclay card and the monarch left a generous tip, then they all entered the pub in their historic past life regalia, two from the England of the Dark Ages, one a Viking marauder. The few day drinkers at the bar gave them a serious double-take. One bottle blond lady shook her head, tossed some bills on the counter, pushed off her stool and uttered, "That's it. I'm here-by giving up drinking. These hallucinations of mine are just getting too weird."

Ralph, the establishment's manager, just happened to be at the end of the bar checking the previous day's receipts. He looked up, and spying Irv and Hershel, shouted, "Hey, good to see you... but Halloween is still a few months off, so what's with the very realistic costumes?" Ralph tipped his head toward Thor.

Irv and Hershel got a good laugh out of this while Thor's face clouded in bewilderment.

"It's okay, big man," Hershel told the Viking chieftain, giving him a light punch on the shoulder, "Just a local joke." Then turning to Ralph, the brew pub manager, he asked, "Any chance of borrowing some modern cloths? We weren't expecting to show up here, so we didn't quite dress for the occasion."

Ralph almost doubled over in amusement while Justin, the daytime bartender, kept a serious countenance. "You'll be drinking strong IPA?" the barman asked, pulling three warm glasses from the rack behind the bar. He started pulling the tap to fill the glasses without waiting for a reply. Strong IPA was all these people from elsewhere in time ever seemed to drink.

When Ralph got his mirth under control, he told King Irv, "All I've got is spare cook and waiter outfits, but if you can hang out here for an hour or so, I can send Trixie, the book keeper, down to the Goodwill to do some shopping. Do you know what sizes you wear?"

"Sizes?" Irv asked with a puzzled expression. Thor just looked on, as though he had swallowed a pigeon.

"Oh yeah, right," Ralph demurred. "You wouldn't know anything about modern sizes for clothes. How about I have Trixie measure you and then she'll go shopping."

Ralph looked around his brew pub at the gawking day drinkers. "And maybe you could wait upstairs in the special events room. I think you might be scaring some of my regulars."

Hershel, Irv and Thor carried their drinks up the stairs to the large private room where Ralph locked the door behind them. "Trixie will be right with you. I'll be back with some civilian clothes before you know it," he shouted over his shoulder to the secured door.

CHAPTER EIGHTEEN

Trixie entered the room shortly with another round of strong ale and a plastic tape measure. She draped her tape across each man in turn, using three separate pages of her spiral-bound diary to record the time traveler's measurements.

She gave Thor's biceps a squeeze commenting, "My, you are a big one, aren't you? Eighteen inches!" With a wink, she then mumbled something about a date if they were still here Saturday, her night off. King Irv dismissed the girl with a scowl and they returned to their drinking.

As they were tossing down the dregs of their third round, Trixie came back into the room carrying more ale and two large plastic bags.

"Show time," she called with a wide grin. "Let's see what we've got here." Trixie set the tray of drinks on the table then turned to the bags draped over her arm.

Pivoting to King Irv, she pulled a nice pair of khaki slacks and a green cable-knit sweater from one of her bags. "You can just pull the sweater over your royal tunic, majesty, and no one will ever guess." She punctuated her statement with a nervous chuckle.

Then, focusing her gaze on Hershel, she brought out a pair of Levis with torn knees and a long sleeved Pendleton wool shirt in a red and blue checked pattern. Hershel nodded his approval. He suddenly remembered Melissa, the lady he'd met when procuring wine grapes for King Irv's winemakers some years earlier. Melissa would be impressed with his outfit if he could find a way to stop up in the wine country and visit her.

"And you, big fellah," Trixie winked at Thor. "This really cool black leather jacket didn't come cheap, but I put some of my own greenbacks into it 'cause it is so *you*." She withdrew a jacket from the third bag that had a motorcycle club logo embroidered on the back along with a pair of greasy black stovepipe pants.

"You don't need a shirt," she swooned. "The pants and jacket say it all. If only I could get you a Harley to ride." Trixie's eyes rolled back dreamily.

Thor's bewildered face swept around the room. What was this pretty girl going on about? How he wished he could be back home in the Hardanger Fjord where life was simple and straight forward.

Trixie approached him again, gave his upper arm another squeeze and then planted a big kiss on his cheek. "Remember me, big boy," she uttered softly with a wink. She turned to leave the room and let these time travel strangers put on their new clothes.

When they'd changed into their more up-to-date gear, Ralph unlocked the door and allowed them downstairs to the main bar, where he served them hamburgers.

"You'll love these, uh, sandwiches, I believe they're called," King Irv told the Viking, "One of my favorite treats whenever I come to this point in time."

At least Thor was relieved that he could pick the thing up and eat it with his hands. Those knife and fork things Queen Sophie had expected him to use back at Warehouse Castle had almost driven him crazy.

"After we've eaten," Thor asked King Irv, "What about my ship and my crew?"

"And what about my safe passage back to the Wholesale Kingdom," Irv countered. "We're on my turf now, old son," he laughed, "But we'll stay here for a few days. I think you'll enjoy this future time… And your men should be fine, sequestered though they may be on your ship.

"Maybe tomorrow Hershel can take you to the beach. King Arthur's Merlin from Old England found the beach to be quite amusing."

Hershel slapped his forehead with his open left palm. "No, Irv, not the beach. Don't you remember the trouble I had with King Arthur's man when we visited the beach? All those scantily clothed babes…"

Irv laughed. "I don't think our Viking friends are from such a repressive society as Arthurs," he told his man of magic. "Though I could be wrong," he added with a wink, just to get Hershel stirred up.

CHAPTER NINETEEN

Ralph once again secured rooms for his time traveling guests at the Motel Eight, just down the street from his Metaphysical Brewery. He booked King Irv a room all his own while securing a room with two double beds for Hershel and the Viking chieftain.

Thor was fascinated by television. He couldn't figure out the news broadcasts, but he loved the golf channel, fishing shows and the comedies where people did silly things and everyone laughed. The Viking held firm control of the remote as he lay back on his soft, clean bed. He simply grunted every time Hershel tried to speak with him.

After an hour, the frustrated Merlin decided to introduce Thor to the room's mini-bar. Hershel brought forth a one ounce flask of Bacardi, unscrewing the top and presenting it to his roommate.

At first, Thor waved the tiny bottle away, his attention firmly focused on an old rerun of **My Mother the Car** with Jerry Van Dyke. Hershel climbed onto Thor's bed, insinuating himself into the Viking's field of vision, and mimed pouring the contents of the small bottle down his throat. When he finally had Thor's attention, he offered the small bottle of rum and again pretended to pour something into his mouth, then he mimed acting silly.

The Viking's eyes widened and he took the proffered plastic flask. He sucked the small bottle dry, made a face, and then set his eyes to bore into those of King Irv's Merlin. A minute passed, then two… And Thor's eyes widened and his head shook a positive up and down.

Hershel went to the small refrigerator and extracted another Bacardi, but Thor extended an arm past the Merlin and grabbed two miniatures of blended Scotch Whiskey. Thor quickly twisted the caps off both bottles and downed them in one swallow each, then turned to Hershel with a broad smile. "Thor likes!" he roared.

By midnight, the mini-bar was empty and Thor was snoring loudly. Hershel wondered what he might tell his king in the morning. How would they be able to deal with a drunk of Thor's size or the hangover the man would have?

But when Hershel awoke, sun streaming in the windows of their room, he could hear water running in the room's shower… And the large Viking singing an unrecognizable tune at full volume.

Hershel shook his head. This could prove to be an interesting day, he told himself. Pulling a robe provided by the hotel around himself, Hershel put the magnetic room key in his pocket and headed next door to speak with his Monarch.

"Ah, highness," he called to the back of his king, who was sitting in a chair staring out the window over the ghetto streets of Oakland.

King Irv caught his eye in a mirror close by the window. The monarch gave a weary sigh. "I know," he replied. "As if King Arthur and his entourage wasn't enough, now we have this Viking rabble. Honestly, I don't know what to do beyond praying. If only the Rabbi was here, close at hand. I'm sure he would have the answer."

"Ah, so what are we suppose to do, highness?" the Merlin asked.

"We'll just amuse this Viking man as best we can until we can find an opening to break free from his spell," King Irv sighed. "For now, simply keep him entertained. Take him to the beach, to see the big bridges of this modern land and whatever else we can find while we figure out how to fix your time travel invention and get us home. What else can we do?"

CHAPTER TWENTY

Meanwhile, back at the Alameda Marina on San Francisco Bay, some two-dozen Viking sailors were getting antsy. They could feel the motion that told them they were on the water, but they were somehow enclosed within the cabin of an unfamiliar vessel. The only man allowed on deck was the English fisherman, Miles, who could speak the language if anyone from the present day should question their presence.

When the Viking crew got bored with their sequestering, four of the men managed to break down a flimsy wooden door to get the run of the ship, but they were confused by the narrow passageways and the many small cabins along these hallways. Up on deck, Miles could hear their destruction and shuddered at the thought of the Norwegian's escaping into the modern world. He'd been warned that his friends from Thor's crew would not be able to handle modern times. He could barely deal with it himself, and that was after King Irv had explained everything to him.

Fram, one of the more inquisitive Vikings, poked around the below-deck area. He tapped around for hollow surfaces and stuck his head into every storage locker or tight space. After an hour or so of his exploits, Fram found one of the kegs of ale that had been brewed aboard their ship while they sat along the banks of the Mississippi. It was in a small closet at the very rear of the boat. The keg was untapped and weighed so much he knew it had to be filled to the brim, even if it wasn't very good ale.

Bunging out the cork and helping himself to a generous tankard of the alcohol, Fram stumbled back along the passageway to alert his fellow sailors to what he'd found. Soon, the entire crew was lined up, dried-out old bull's horns in their outstretched hands as mugs, to get a horn full of ale.

His mind cleared by a generous drink or two, Bjorn, Norwegian for Bear, was the first man to find the ladder that could take him up on the yacht's open deck, but his ale horn was nearly exhausted. He ventured back down, refreshed his drink, then hammered his way through the hatch cover and went topside to explore. He walked slowly along the stearboard side of the vessel, fascinated by the tall castles he saw lining the shore and the mountains behind them. He also noted that there were some kind of small things on wheels traveling very fast just beyond the place where they were docked. When he reached the vessel's bow, he turned and continued down the port side, weaving a little from the strong ale and staring out across the waters of San Francisco Bay to more very tall castles along the distant shore.

Just across the narrow dock from Thor's Viking ship was moored another large yacht, much like what Hershel had turned the appearance of their boat into, owned by a wealthy San Francisco real estate mogul. The man had a daughter currently attending the University of California at Berkeley. As the man himself was out of town on business, his daughter, Darlene, was throwing a sort of impromptu party aboard daddy's yacht.

Darlene had come up on deck to smoke a cigarette, something that was proclaimed to be against the big boat's rules. She figured below deck it would leave a trace odor that Daddy would discover and she'd never hear the end of it.

The party, however, was supposed to remain down in the ship's salon, so that none of the neighbors in the marina could rat her out to mummy and daddy. She was taking a huge chance coming out on deck for a smoke and she knew it… Then suddenly, she saw Bjorn in his bearskin drape, horned helmet and bare muscled arms exposed beneath his bright red beard and long blond hair. The man's biceps had to be twenty inches around, she marveled. Even from across the narrow wharf, she was mesmerized by the man's dazzling blue eyes.

She stood there staring for how long, she didn't know. Bjorn stared back at her with a broad grin showing bad teeth. Bjorn was sure that he was in love, but was it with a real girl or some strange phantom created by this English fellow's time travel thingy? They continued to silently stare at each other.

After about ten minutes, Darlene's boyfriend, Tom, came up the ladder to see what had happened to the love of his young life. He walked up behind Darlene, put an arm around her waist, and then followed her gaze to the rough-looking chap on the neighboring vessel with an evil looking broad sword hanging from his waist.

"Baby, like, we'd better get out of here," he breathed into her left ear. "This guy looks like trouble."

Darlene let out a ginormous sigh. "Oh, yes, doesn't he?" she breathed. "Oh yes, trouble!"

As Tom tried to pull her back to the vessel's hatch, he bumped into his best friend, Wayde, who had followed him and was advancing up the ladder. Wayde looked past Tom and Darlene, saw Bjorn and shouted, "Hey, guys! Toga party, come up and check this out, furry animal skin togas."

Thor's well cloaked Viking ship was, in an instant, stormed by well-bred college students and a few intellectual hangers-on carrying twelve-ounce red plastic cups. One or two of the kids made their way down and discovered the Viking's keg of strong ale, where they stood in line with the Norwegian sailors for a sample.

Other Cal students brought over cans of Budweiser and quart bottles of Stone's Arrogant Bastard Ale, which they traded freely with the Norsemen for horns of the old Viking brew. The party was out in the open and spreading across two yachts and a long stretch of the private marina's dock space.

Åke Hansen, a Danish student from Berkeley's History department, recognized the language the Viking's were speaking and started conversing with them. He was very curious how they came to be on a big cruiser in San Francisco Bay, but the Old Norwegian sailors were as much in the dark as Åke was. Åke was quickly recruited by Darlene, who very much wanted to talk to Bjorn. She offered him money, or even her favors, if he would act as an interpreter. Åke thought that was a hoot and quickly agreed.

The college boys, being college boys, had invited plenty of college girls to Darlene's boat. Some of these young debutants were terrified of the Viking marauders, but others, like Darlene, were fascinated by these rough *real* men. One of the non-students made a phone call to a friend, who was a member of a local motorcycle club, to brag about the strong ale on this party boat, and soon the roar of Harley Davidson's could be heard coming down the wharf.

The bikers started fist fights all along the wharf back to the marina office. Vikings, having few inhibitions, had some of the young and very drunk coeds shedding their skirts and sweaters just before dawn. Anyone still awake around the marina had an eyeful of this orgy across time. College girls from the early twenty-first century were taking tall, sturdy lovers from a thousand years before, while drunken fraternity boys and motorcycle outlaws lay passed out on the decks of two yachts and a narrow, wooden finger of dock space.

CHAPTER TWENTY-ONE

King Irv's cat, Bird, observed all this from his place on the yacht's yardarm. "No good can come of this," he thought to himself, then, "If only Irv would return right now to nip this craziness in the bud." He pressed his head down flat on the yardarm, closed his eyes and crossed his paws over the top of his ears. "Hear no evil, see no evil."

But his king didn't return. Irv was busy, along with Thor and his Merlin, Hershel, watching an old Errol Flynn pirate movie on the Motel 8's pay-per-view television channel. Irv had gone to Hershel and Thor's room to check up on them and had become interested in the old film on the room's TV screen.

Every now and then, Thor would loudly mumble, "Where do they get such giant ships?" or "What are these things that spit out fire and iron balls?"

At each such outburst, Hershel would shush the Viking and nod his head toward the large screen of the television. There was nothing worse than trying to follow the thread of a good story when someone who didn't even speak the language well kept interrupting.

As they watched Errol Flynn leap from the rigging, his sword carving a path through a wall of human flesh, they sipped blended Scotch whisky from the motel room's replenished mini bar. It was almost becoming a routine for Hershel, who often traveled from

Wholesale Kingdom to the future. King Irv didn't like time travel, but felt safe in the company of his very clever Merlin.

Thor, however, felt very insecure and out of place. He was the undisputed champion on the battlefield, raiding new lands, or even in ship-to-ship combat, but he was at a total loss getting drunk in some big future city and then watching *others* fighting through some large window-like thing in a small room with two wide soft beds. Oh, how he wished he could be back in Hardangerfjord, slopping the pigs at his father's farm.

When the movie ended, Thor looked around the room. Hershel was snoring loudly, his mouth hanging open. King Irv was turned away from him, sleeping on his side, and Thor had to pee, really badly. Just before he let loose, he remembered the little room near the front door of their chamber where he'd been told he should use a white bowl thing for bodily functions. He pushed himself off the bed and made his way to the small space where he could relieve himself without anyone looking down on him.

After peeing for a long time, he lay back down on the room's wide, king-size bed, but he couldn't sleep. So many new and wondrous things he'd seen over the past day. So much that challenged his mind. Could all this be real? Or was this all a strange dream? He was just beginning to nod off when he heard a loud, intermittent buzzing sound from the small table between their beds.

King Irv turned over with a loud groan and grabbed a small, strange thing from atop the table. Then, even weirder, he talked to this little white box as though speaking to another person.

After a few sentences, King Irv was sitting straight up, wide awake, and shaking Hershel with his free hand. While he spoke to this white box thing, Irv occasionally would cover it with his hand and mumble, "Oh shit."

When he finally put the box back into a small white dish thing on the table, he shouted, "Hershel, we've got big trouble. We'd better get a hold of Ralph, right away!"

CHAPTER TWENTY-TWO

As the sun was peaking over Mount Diablo and the Black Hills to the east, the Alameda Police began raiding the local marina. They'd had reports of public fornication, rapes, vandalism, public drunkenness and men brandishing swords along the docks. They hesitated briefly, as one of the boats in question was the yacht of Stan Shacly, one of the Bay area's top real estate brokers and a strong supporter of the community, including the Police and Sheriff's League, but in the end, they decided that they'd better at least check it out.

And check it out they did, with the local SWAT team and three carloads of regular officers. They quickly spotted Darlene Shacly and told her to skedaddle before they made any arrests, but Darlene, her bra hanging out beneath her expensive Hermes top and her panties around her ankles, said she chose to stay and defend her new lover, Bjorn. "Arrest me if you must," she told the sergeant. "I'm sure father will provide a lawyer to defend me and my new friends."

The police contingent stopped in their tracks to think about this. No one wanted to get on the bad side of Stan Shacly. They began a retreat, but quickly received a radio call from the Alameda Chief. Shacly had been called and he swore that there was no one authorized to be aboard his yacht.

"Arrest them all," the real estate man had told the chief. "If my daughter is with them, arrest her too. It might serve to teach her a lesson about obeying me. We can always wipe out any criminal record on her part," he told them emphatically, "can we not?"

And so Darlene Shacly was cuffed along with Bjorn, Åke and all the Viking men and college hanger's on. An Alameda Sheriff's Department bus hauled them to the county lock up where the night crew, only minutes away from getting off duty, began to process them.

The officers and admins from the night shift were not happy. Most of them were exhausted from a long busy twelve hour stint. Others were just plain tired. They all looked at the men exiting the paddy wagon in their bear skin tunics with un-confiscated swords by their sides and knew instantly that this would be a long, drawn-out process, taking most of the day to deal with these characters.

At eight in the morning, the oncoming shift was told to help them, but everyone was so swamped that it didn't do much good. None of the men in bearskins had any kind of identification, along with the fact that they spoke a strange tongue no one at the deten-tion center could fathom. One of the toga dressed primitives spoke something close to English, but everything he told them was so out-rageous he had to be certifiably crazy. Time travel from a thousand years before? No, this had to be part of some grave, anti-American conspiracy. It was a shame that Stan Shacly's daughter had to be caught up in such a scandal.

The Vikings were disarmed of their swords, hammers and oth-er weapons. They were herded into the county drunk tank as there wasn't another single cell large enough to accommodate them all. After considering his options, the sheriff shoved the drunken male college student in after the Northmen. The coeds and sorority girls they stashed down the hall in another wing of vacant lock-ups. It was decided that they would wait until the mayor arrived in his office Monday morning before any further action was taken. The most important thing now was to try and keep the press away from this total balls-up.

Darlene found herself in a special cell. It appeared to be more like a motel room. In fact, it *was* a motel room although she didn't know it. Upon her father's orders, the Alameda Police had placed the coed in a room at the Oakland Motel 8, the room next door to King Irv and down the hall from Hershel and Thor. They placed a very senior patrolman in the hall outside as a guard until Stan Shacly could come for his daughter.

Darlene kept screaming that she wanted to see her new boyfriend, Bjorn, but there was no one listening outside her door besides Patrolman Quertz, who was nearly deaf and just waiting out his last six months to full retirement. The wealthy coed kept shouting that she wanted someone to provide a lawyer for Bjorn, the man who'd touched her like no man before and who she wanted to marry as soon as they could both be freed from this unfair incarceration.

Darlene's voice was loud, shrill and piercing. While Patrolman Quertz couldn't hear her that well, the girl's voice penetrated the thin walls of the motel. Thor, who was now wide awake, recognized the name of his young sail rigger, Bjorn, whom someone was shouting out. How many people in the modern world would have a name like Bjorn? It had to be that young sailor who was like a son to him. As soon as that crazy English king and his man of magic returned, he would demand that they seek out this distressed lady and help to free his man, Bjorn.

CHAPTER TWENTY-THREE

King Irv made an international call to his son-in-law, Rutherford, seeking help. "I have lots of connections among the Thames Valley constabulary here in Oxford," his daughter's husband told Irv, "but I haven't a clue about the police in America. They're a very different bunch. Ralph would be your best bet on this situation." Rutherford gave King Irv a list of phone numbers with which he might reach the manager of the Metaphysical Brewing Company.

After half a dozen calls, the monarch finally located Ralph, who was spending the night with Trixie, his book keeper.

The first thing Ralph said, when he realized who was calling was, "Oh my God. You won't rat me out to Emma, will you?" Emma was Ralph's girl friend of many years, the lady that had first helped connect him with King Irv's entourage and had been responsible for Ralph setting up his San Francisco micro brewery in the first place.

"I didn't hear any of that," King Irv replied in a serious tone although laughter was so close to his voice he could barely contain it. Along the phone line, he could sense a deep exhale of relief from both Ralph and his new lady friend.

"It would seem," the Jewish monarch began again, "that some of Thor's Vikings... you remember Thor don't you? Viking chap we brought into the brewery yesterday? Well, his crew whom we'd stashed away in the Alameda Marina made friends with some others along the docks. They had a big party and, well, they're all in the nick as of this morning. I think we may require your help in getting them out again."

There was a long pause across the phone line. Finally, Ralph asked, "They were dressed in some of those Salvation Army clothes that Trixie provided, right?"

"Unfortunately, no," King Irv told him, while Hershel fumed in the background. "They were in their battle dress of bear skins and leather shields. Apparently, some of them brandished swords at the arresting officers." He could almost feel Ralph cringing through the telephone wires.

"And Rutherford?" came the weak voice through the line.

"...Told us to call you and you could help to sort it out."

There was another long pause on the line. In a voice muffled, as though someone was holding a hand over the instrument, Irv heard, "Jesus, I could lose my license over this... I could lose everything!"

Just to keep the conversation from stalling, Irv told him, "I'm sure Rutherford can get it all sorted in the long run. Right now, we need to get these Vikings out of gaol and back through time."

A brighter voice now came through the receiver. "Yes. Sneak your time travel thing into the jail and send them all away. It's the perfect solution, why didn't you think of this?"

King Irv handed the receiver to Hershel, who had been listening on speaker phone. "Ah, Ralph?" the Merlin said. "We've got a little problem here. One of these Viking guys put a sword through my time machine, so for the moment, it's out of commission. We're kinda like, stuck here. So, don't you know anyone among the locals who can help us get our men out of gaol?"

It was difficult to tell if the sound coming through the telephone line was the tearing of hair, gnashing of teeth or just someone jumping up and down on the instrument in question. After about five minutes, Trixie came on the line.

"Ralph is very upset. I think he might be having a stroke or something. His eyes are bulging out and he's sweating like a stuck hog. Can he call you back later? I mean if he lives?"

CHAPTER TWENTY-FOUR

The Alameda County Deputy Public Defender, Sid Fox, who was on duty Sunday morning answered the very weird summons from Sheriff's Sergeant Mulvane, about a dozen men or more dressed in animal skins with no identification who had been arrested for public drunkenness and other crimes just hours ago. As Counselor Fox was the newest man in the department, only six months out of law school, he figured it was probably another jape, part of the ongoing hazing he was enduring from his fellows in the county offices.

Still, he knew he had to answer the call. Joke or not, they would harass him to no end if he didn't come down to the courthouse to answer their request. He was sure he'd been had when the clerk, an older woman in a white blouse, long brown skirt and sensible shoes, with dark eyes and grey hair pulled into a tight bun, started telling him about his prospective defendants being relieved of broad swords, leather shields and heavy iron hammers. She kept a straight face.

Sid Fox went into the lockup to confront Sergeant Mulvane wearing a broad grin. "Come on," he chuckled, "are you going to tell me we've been invaded by an army of Vikings or something?"

Without cracking a smile, Mulvane turned on his heel and led Fox down the institutional green hallway to the drunk tank where the wild miscreants awaited. "You speak any Scandinavian languages?" the sergeant asked over his shoulder.

Fox's laughter turned to a nervous giggle when he saw the detainees, some seated on the floor, others hanging on the bars, and one or two throwing punches at each other in the rear of the large cell.

"What," Fox asked, "did you guys raid a theater company or something? What kinda gag is this, anyway?"

Still serious faced, Mulvane turned and told him, "No theater, no joke, Sid. We were called out to a loud, drunken party at the marina. We found these guys hanging around on Stan Shacly's yacht and someone else's boat moored next to it. You know about Shacly, right? One of these characters was trying to molest Shacly's daughter. Whyn't you see if you can get anything out of them. As it is, we probably can't even set bail until we know who they are or where they came from. The sheriff is trying to find someone out at Cal Berkeley who speaks Norwegian who can act as an interpreter for us."

Sid Fox bravely entered the tank. "Hey, guys," he squeaked, "Anyone here know any English?" His words, along with his timid demeanor, drew loud guffaws and taunts from the bearded ruffians. Fox cleared his throat and with a little more chutzpa in his voice, he tried again, "Anyone?"

After a few nervous heartbeats, the sea of hairy men parted to allow a shorter man through. This new spokesperson wore the tattered remnants of a green sweater, homemade khaki pants so old they bore a threadbare shine, and a weathered flat tweed cap.

"I'm somewhat proficient in the Queen's tongue," the man told Sid Fox in a heavily accented voice. "How can I be of service to you?"

Fox fell back onto a hard wood bench and began to stutter, "Ha, ha, who are ya, you pe, pe, people? Wha, where did you come from? Ha, how did you ga, get here?"

Miles glanced up to the exposed pipes along the low ceiling. "I only wish I knew the answer to that," he smiled.

"Dah, dah, what do you mean 'you wish you knew?' You *must* have come from somewhere?" Now a hint of anger crept into the young attorney's voice. "Explain yourselves," he demanded, opening his briefcase and taking out a pen and yellow legal pad.

Miles doffed his cap, held it in both hands in front of his protruding belly. "Well, sir, me personally? Me mates and I was fishing and our boat capsized. I was about to give it all up and let the sea take me life, as it had me two partners, when this mob come along in a long ship with a dragon's head on the bow."

"Here in San Francisco Bay?" Fox breathed over a rapidly dropping jaw.

"Heavens no," Miles laughed. "We was in the North Sea, just off Tweedmouth."

"Tweedmouth," the lawyer parroted, "in the North Sea..."

"Righty-oh mate." Miles nodded his head for emphasis. "I mean I can't say just how *far* off from Old Blighty we'd drifted. We might-a been closer to the Dutch Coast. We was kinda lost."

"Dutch Coast," came the attorney's confused voice again. He gave his noggin a vigorous shake, then went on, "And then you sailed halfway around the world to get here? With a bunch of heathen Vikings?"

"Haven't a clue how we got *here*," Miles chuckled. "You was asking me where I came from and I told you."

"So you were on a Viking ship? What happened then?"

"You ain't gonna believe this, Gov," the English sailor chuckled louder.

"Try me," Sid Fox barked. "Just tell me and I'll make up my own mind."

"Well, sir," Miles drawled, "We was kinda lifted across time. We was in my time first, if you please, then we was many years earlier, way back in what I could only guess was the Dark Ages, then we came ahead to the future, and then back a few more years, and suddenly, here we are." Miles winked at the Deputy Public Defender, who began shaking his head rapidly once more and wiggling his little pinky in his left ear.

"Is there anyone else here who could speak with me, anyone who might be able to explain this more clearly?"

"Our Captain, Thor, might be able to help," Miles told him with a grin.

"And which one of these men is Thor?"

"Sorry mate," Miles told him, looking more serious now. "Thor went ashore with some magician from very old England and his ruler, King Irving. They put some spell on our ship to make it look different from what it is then they just kinda, you know, went out for a little stroll from which they ain't returned yet."

"King Irving?" Fox repeated, "I've always been a student of the history of England and I've never heard of a King Irving."

"He's the Jewish king," Miles told him with another wink and a nod.

CHAPTER TWENTY-FIVE

At just after 9:00 am, Irv, Hershel and Thor were getting ready to head downstairs at their motel to partake of the free breakfast when the phone rang. It was a much calmer Ralph who greeted King Irv through the line.

"My lawyer, who handles all the brewery business, said he isn't all that good at criminal law, but he has a partner who could maybe help us. When I explained about Vikings from somewhere else in time, he first told me he loves a challenge, then he confessed that it wouldn't be cheap. He wants to charge us double-time to help, especially if Stan Shacly's daughter is involved."

"You know Rutherford is good for it, whatever it might cost," Irv told the distressed pub owner. "We've somehow got to get these Vikings out of gaol so Hershel can fix his time travel machine and we can get back home to Warehouse Castle again."

"Whatever you say, Irv," Ralph told him in a voice that betrayed the bar owner had taken some kind of drugs to cope with this stressful situation. "Do you want to meet this lawyer guy here at the brewery just after lunch time? I know you and Hershel could make a good case to present to this guy, but I'm not sure if I would recommend bringing Thor along. He might just be a little too much for this attorney fellow to handle."

"We'll be there for lunch," King Irv told Ralph, "so that we won't be late for the start of the meeting. I'll have a little talk with Hershel to decide if we should bring Thor or not."

"I'll reserve you a private room upstairs," Ralph assured the monarch.

The attorney Ralph introduced to King Irv and Hershel was a man in his mid-thirties, Rolf Andreson, a big, broad-shouldered man with bright red hair and a short red beard. Of obvious Norwegian heritage, Andreson could have passed for one of the men he was being hired to defend if he wasn't wearing a very expensive, hand-made, wool suit.

Andreson listened attentively to the unlikely tale Irv and Hershel spun before him. Thor sat quietly off to the side sipping strong ale and nodding agreement from time to time. Hershel had asked the Viking captain to refrain from comment unless he or King Irv specifically asked for his input.

Hershel spoke first, giving some background by explaining how he had, back in old England, invented first a solar panel to provide energy, and then his small tin vehicle containing another quartz-powered device which could transport people across time. He told about how he'd met Rutherford, and Rutherford had gifted him with the big round globe that allowed him to program his device to easily traverse space as well as time.

When they got down to the nitty and gritty, it became just a bit more confusing, the idea of the same time machine existing in future history, after the Hershel now seated before the attorney had died, in his own time. But Hershel still lived, by virtue of his travels across the ages. It took much of the afternoon and three rounds of strong ale before everyone seemed to understand the full background of the current situation.

Then they had to confront the dilemma facing them. A Viking ship, disguised as an expensive yacht was moored in a very hoity-toity marina carrying a crew from one thousand years before who had hosted a party for local college students and motorcycle outlaws.

Of course no one had identification, none of the sailors out of history at least. Counselor Andreson quickly came up with the same solution Ralph had proposed; simply send everyone back through time to where they belonged.

Over yet another round of strong ale, Hershel explained how one of the Viking sailors had put his time machine out of commission and the discussion returned back to square one.

With his head spinning from strong drink, Rolf Andreson doodled on his yellow legal pad, writing "John Doe one through twenty-two" halfway down the page, followed by "Hopeless," underlined three times.

CHAPTER TWENTY-SIX

Around four that afternoon, a rather tipsy Rolf Andreson stopped by the Alameda County Courthouse to file a motion to have the Viking sailors released on their own recognizance. In his brief, he cited that the twenty-two sailors were foreign nationals, simply passing through the Port of San Francisco on route to some farther destination. He proposed that his clients, through him, would gladly pay fines to the court for their indiscretions, the amount of the fines to be set by the courts.

The clerk read his brief and asked, in a sarcastic tone, "So what nation are these seaman registered in? Surely they must carry papers from whatever nation they call home?"

"Urm, it's a very small kingdom," Rolf improvised. "So few people live there that no one has ever required them to undergo such formalities." Even as he said it, he realized how ridiculous it sounded, but he struggled to keep his slightly tipsy face straight.

"And that nation is?" the clerk persisted.

"Ah, it's called Valhalla?" Rolf replied, on the verge of a giggle.

"Valhalla?" the clerk said with a suspicious look. Isn't that some kind of mythical Scandinavian afterworld?"

"That's what the place is named for," Rolf told him, suppressing a grin.

"I don't think so," the clerk told him. "If you can't produce some kind of IDs for these guys, they'll rot here forever. Why don't you call the embassy of this *Valhalla* place and have them send us some paperwork, then we'll get a bail hearing set."

Rolf gave the clerk a dubious look, then turned to leave. "And you'd better call a cab to take you home," the court clerk hollered at his back. "Your breath could get a team of footballers high."

Rolf ignored the clerk's suggestion and drove himself back to the Metaphysical Brewing Company where he reported his encounter to Ralph. "His Highness and the Merlin are still upstairs," the bar owner told him. "I'm sure they'll want to hear what you've found."

Rolf stumbled up the stairs to the conference room where he found King Irv, Hershel and Thor feasting on onion rings smothered in ketchup and downing more strong ale.

"The court wants to see identification for all your boys," Rolf told them, motioning for a waitress just outside the room to bring him an ale. "Do you know anyone who could maybe make up some false papers?"

"False papers?" King Irv asked with knitted brows. "What are false papers?"

"Like those passport and drivers license thingies Rutherford's cousins provided us," Hershel told his monarch. "But I don't think we could get passports and drivers licenses for all Thor's men. That would be quite a tall order."

The Merlin thought for another minute, then continued, "It would take too long anyway."

Ralph, who was just entering the room, exclaimed, "Don't even think about it. That's all I need is having some kind of forgery rap sent my way. Can't you just do something with your time machine?"

Hershel simply rolled his eyes heavenward. Rolf, their attorney took a long pull of ale and slowly began to slide from his chair onto the floor.

CHAPTER TWENTY-SEVEN

Ralph called a taxi for the attorney. By the time the cab arrived, Rolf was semi-conscious once more. King Irv and Hershel stood him between them and marched him to the back door, where they poured him into a Bay Area Yellow Cab. Ralph fished the lawyer's wallet from his coat pocket to get an address where the cabbie might drop him off. He also extracted one of the lawyer's credit cards for payment, requesting that the taxi driver slip it back into his fare's pocket, along with a receipt, when they reached their destination. As it was a warm, pleasant evening, Irv, Thor and Hershel walked back to their motel.

After partaking of the motel's free breakfast again the next morning, Hershel rented a car so that they might do some sightseeing as long as they were stuck here. When the agency brought a bright yellow Fiat around, Hershel shoe-horned Thor into the rear seat while King Irv opened the passenger side door and got in. They drove across the Oakland Bay Bridge and then made a circuit of the City by the Bay. Hershel took them to Fisherman's Wharf, then down Lombard Street, the crookedest street in the world, and finally down along the coast. By late afternoon, Hershel parked them behind the Metaphysical Brewery and they went inside for lunch.

As things were fairly quiet and the trio seemed well behaved, Ralph let them sit downstairs in the main bar where they could talk to people. The three had burgers and pint glasses of strong ale while they sat and watched a football match on the bar television.

Arsenal was one point ahead of Real Madrid and all three of the time travelers were fascinated by the game.

"You know we Vikings invented this football game," Thor remarked in passing.

Ralph, standing nearby, overheard the Viking chieftain and walked down the bar to the trio.

"Vikings invented football?" he posed to Thor. "I find that hard to believe. Explain yourself."

Thor gave a deep, throaty laugh. "My uncle, Trygve, was on one of the first boats to land in Ireland," he told them. Trygve noticed right away that everyone deferred to the priest of their Christian church before they made any move. So, Trygve told his men to behead this priest fellow, which sent these Irishmen into a frenzy. When they lopped the chap's head off, they all went into a scramble, we later learned that they believed they had to retrieve the man's head and bury it with the body so that his so-called soul could travel to their mythical heaven place.

"Anyway, our Viking crew had a grand old time for the afternoon and long into the night kicking this man's head about and keeping it from these Irish churchmen. When the daylight faded, the Irish churchmen ignited torches all around the field to keep the match going. The Irish chaps finally reclaimed their priest's head late in the night and buried it. Thinking back the next day, they found that they'd had such a good time that they made an effigy of the head from leather stuffed with feathers and resumed the game."

"That has got to be bullshit," Ralph hollered, just a little too loudly. Heads turned all across the main bar of the Metaphysical

Brewery. Thor just grinned at Ralph with knowing eyes. King Irv and Hershel stayed out of the argument.

As they sat drinking while things settled down, Hershel noticed a man two barstools along staring at him. He had a thick head of dark hair, a pointed and graying beard and a big smile. Hershel turned to stare back at the chap and the man moved his drink closer and introduced himself.

"Verne's the name, Jules Verne," the stranger told him in a strongly accented voice. "You look like a time traveler sir, am I right?"

Hershel's jaw dropped as he elbowed Irv. "Highness, check this guy out," he whispered out of the corner of his mouth. "What gives?"

The stranger chuckled. "I guess that confirms my suspicions. But don't panic, I am a time traveler as well. I'm so happy to meet some like-minded fellows, and you are?"

Thor's gaze never left the television. He continued to munch his burger and drink his ale. King Irv half turned on his stool but only gave the stranger a quick once-over.

"Ah, Irv?" Hershel queried his monarch. "Do we know this guy?"

"No, you probably don't know me," the stranger continued, "Unless you're avid readers here in these future times."

"Avid readers?" Irv tossed back, becoming more interested in the conversation.

"Of books," Verne replied, "readers of books… well, I can see that you're not. But I sense that you are not from these times and you probably have some kind of time travel machine stashed near-by, am I right? Its okay, I have one myself. So can we talk? You are?" he pressed.

After a long pause, King Irv gave a furtive look around the room and then extended his right hand.

"King Irving David," he smiled, "of the Wholesale Kingdom… but that's some years in the past. We are a Hebrew monarchy in very old England."

"Ah, Irv," Hershel cautioned, "We don't know anything about this guy. Are we sure he isn't someone trying to bust Thor's sailors?"

"Thor's sailors?" Verne gave a puzzled look. "And would this red bearded fellow sitting on your left be Thor then? And is he from old England too?"

Thor turned from the big screen over the bar at the mention of his name. He looked Verne over top-to-bottom then asked Irv, "This man friend of yours?"

Ralph, overhearing some of the conversation, came down the bar and hovered nervously. 'I don't need any more trouble in my bar,' he was thinking to himself.

Jules Verne waved Ralph away. "We are fine, patròn," he told Ralph. "I'll sig-i-nal when we need something and then maybe I'll buy a round or two for my new friends."

Ralph quickly turned on his heel and departed.

Hershel swiveled his head between the old Viking and the Frenchman, at a loss for words. Irv stepped in.

"Not yet sure if this man is friend or foe," he relayed to Thor, while Verne interrupted with, "A friend, I assure you."

The four men each leaned back to check each other out in the mirror behind the bar. King Irv broke the stalemate. "Well, obviously, we are not from around here, but we are not all travelers from the same point in, what did you say? Time? Our friend Thor comes from much later in years than Hershel and I, but somehow ended up on our shores in our year 4068, just a few months after Passover."

"4068?" Verne spit out incredulously, "But right now we're only in 2012."

"It's that Christian calendar thing again," Hershel laughed, shaking his head. "Why do people want to make things so confusing?" Then turning to Jules Verne, he said, "Don't you know anything about your Torah?"

"I think my ship start out in Christian year 982," Thor nodded, eyes still fixed on the bar TV, "So King Irv must be way earlier." He raised his glass, took a deep draught, and then signaled Ralph for another.

Verne's face showed confusion briefly, then he said, "I get it, yes, you're on the old Jewish calendar that started counting the years in Genesis! But that doesn't help me much... Oh dear."

"Look, it establishes that we're from different places in the fabric of time, okay? So isn't that what you wanted to know in the first place?"

Jules Verne swiveled their direction on his stool, facing his new acquaintances. "So did each of you arrive here in some different, ah, time conveyance?"

"Naw," Hershel chuckled, "we all somehow found ourselves here on Thor's Viking ship, for what it's worth."

CHAPTER TWENTY-EIGHT

The French stranger had to think about this for a moment or two. While he was contemplating things, Ralph came down the bar and tipped his head to the quartet. Verne waved his hand in a positive manner and Ralph brought fresh drinks for all which he put on the Frenchman's tab.

"Let me get this straight," Verne finally spoke. "You all arrived here in San Francisco on a Viking ship from the year 982, but you all came to this location from different places in time? There must be some powerful magic going on here that I am not able to comprehend. King Irv, how did you get on board this Viking boat in the first place?"

"That's easy," Hershel responded, "Thor was ferrying King Irv's family back to modern England after a party at Warehouse Castle."

Now Jules Verne looked more confused than ever. "Ferrying? From a party?"

"My daughter, Princess Judith, wanted to come back through time to have a birthday party for my good queen, Sophie," King Irv told him with a positive nod. "Princess Judith lives in these modern times, probably close to where we are now. Many years ago, when a dark-skinned man from the future came to visit us in old England, my daughter fell in love with the man, married him, and went to live with him in future times. She and her mother, my Queen, bounce back and forward often to stay in touch. I have a lovely granddaughter in these future times, what they call modern day England.

"The Viking ship proved much more convenient for sending them home than Hershel's time contraption which could only seat two people."

Verne tore at his hair. Nothing seemed to be making any sense. The more they told him, the less he understood of it. Were these people all mad? Maybe too much travel across the years did that to people.

"Whoa, hold on," Verne coughed. "Can we back up a minute here?"

Irv, Hershel and Thor all turned to face the Frenchman with blank expressions. "You mean like scoot our chairs back farther into the room?" Irv questioned.

Verne buried his face in his hands. Through his parted fingers, he said, "Let's go back to the start of our conversation. Tell me once more from the top how you all came to be aboard a time-traveling Viking ship. Speak slowly and distinctly, in words that I can understand. If you could tell me in French, it might help.

"Now, you were in this ship going from very old England to modern England. How did Thor's ship end up in very old England and how do you all happen to know each other."

"May I?" Hershel stated, shifting his eyes between King Irv and Thor. "I guess when I died, oh, sometime around 4096, my time travel thingy got covered over by sand or something, like in the sand trap of our golf course. Apparently, it was uncovered by a wind storm a lot of years later and Thor's men found it.

"They pried the guts of my machine out of my vehicle, brought it back to their ship and lashed it to the mast. No one knew what it was but, as I understand it, they were fascinated by the crystals.

Thor set his ale back on the bar and nodded vigorously that this was true.

Hershel continued, "Somehow, one of the Viking sailors must have touched the controls or something, and my old machine sent the ship back through time, setting it into the waters of the North Sea near Warehouse Castle."

"We were unfamiliar with Thor or any of his sailors before this happened," King Irv added. "We had no idea."

Jules Verne's expression remained clouded. "Vikings suddenly appeared in very old England," Verne repeated. "And you could all speak a common tongue?"

Hershel chuckled at this. "That's where Miles comes into the picture."

"Miles," the bewildered Frenchman repeated.

"Miles is English fisherman," Thor stated emphatically. "We rescue him in our own time. He teach us some English."

Verne's eyes passed rapidly between his three companions until King Irv told him, "Miles is an English sailor from Thor's time in history. Thor's men saved him from drowning and he taught them some of our English tongue

"I guess the explanation you're looking for is that we all met across time by virtue of Hershel's time travel thingy, although we weren't really aware of it until you started questioning us."

"Bottom line," Hershel told their inquisitor, "We all somehow got thrown together by the universe and now, here we are in the Metaphysical Brewing Company in modern Oakland, near San Francisco, where you just happened to show up. I think everything happens for a reason, so let's get down to figuring out why we're all here together. Maybe you can help us get Thor's sailors out of the nick and fix my time machine so King Irv and I can get home to very old England and we can all finish happily ever after, as the fairy tales all say.

"These Vikings are warriors, nothing more, nothing less." Verne mused. "You need to leave the thinking to those of us with civilized societies. We are the contemplators and thinkers."

"Someday," Thor told Verne, "my people will become a nation of great thinkers. On our long, dark and lonely nights back in Hardangerfjord, what do we have to do but think?"

Jules Verne took a deep draught of ale and thought about that for another moment. "Well," he drawled, "You may be right, Thor."

Then Verne wiped his lips on the back of his hand, stared at his own image in the bar mirror and spoke again, "I have had some thoughts about a sort of teleportation device, something that could move a room full of people from one location to another. I drew some sketches in my notebook along with mathematical formulas to create such a thing, but I've never had time to work out the full equation or try the idea out…"

"Maybe it's time to try it now," Hershel told him with a penetrating stare.

Meanwhile, back at the Alameda Marina, Bird, King Irv's ginger tabby, was getting very upset. His king and best friend had never left him alone for this long before. He was doing alright, eating mice and seagulls that found their way to the cloaked Viking ship and its neighbors. The sheriff's men guarding the ship had even started leaving some kibbles out for him, along with bowls of fresh water, but he missed his best friend. Had he made his regent, King Irv, jealous when he befriended that red-bearded character? Where could King Irv be and why was he staying away for so long?

CHAPTER TWENTY-NINE

Ralph, working the bar, couldn't help but overhear Verne and Hershel's last interaction. He came down the bar to face them.

"If you've got some kinda Star Trek thing that can beam Thor's crew to another location," he told them, "I might have a location where you could send them.

"The couple who have the farm next door to my parents, one of my former professors, actually, are on sabbatical in Europe for a few months. The guy's son is a good friend of mine. He's house sitting the property while his mom and dad are away."

At this, all the assembled time travelers at the bar became very attentive. "Let me call Jerry," Ralph told them. "I'll invite him to come down to the brewery for a free meal and drinks."

"Can you get him down here now?" Hershel asked, "Like, right away?"

"I'll do my best," Ralph told them. "He's kind of a lonely guy and mildly alcoholic, so it's a good bet he'll come pretty quickly."

"Tell him there're some women here interested in him," Verne suggested with a leer and a nod of his head.

"But that would be a lie," Ralph replied with a concerned face.

"Yeah, but it might speed him up," Hershel grinned. "We can always say they went home after he gets here."

The four time travelers had a couple more rounds and a big plate of nachos while they waited. Thor discovered that he really loved nachos. It was getting on for evening and the brewery started filling up with young drinkers. As they waited, a pair of secretaries came into the brewery. They sat at the bar and started having a conversation when a pair of young men in suits and ties sat by them and started coming on to them. The suits were loud, rude and obnoxious. The ladies were about to abandon their drinks and leave when King Irv became aware of their plight.

"Hershel, old thing," he said to his Merlin. "I believe those overbearing chaps are frightening the young ladies a few seats down from us. Do you think there's anything we can do to help?"

Hershel turned to Thor. "Hey, big guy, can you help out here?"

"What you want Thor to do," the Viking asked with a smile.

"Okay, Thor, listen carefully," Hershel coached. "You go put a hand on each of those smarmy guys' shoulders…"

Thor nodded that he understood.

"Then I want you to make an angry face and say to them, 'Are you bothering my sister?' Got that?"

"I say 'You bothering my sister,' right?"

"Close enough," Hershel grinned. "You know the term 'menacing?'"

When Thor looked confused, Hershel bared his teeth and growled loudly.

The Viking's face brightened. "Menacing, yes!"

The big Viking slid his barstool back and sauntered down to where the secretaries were gathering their purses to go. He cocked his head for a few seconds as though he might be listening to their conversation. He then put a tight grip on the shoulders of the two suits, squeezing their bodies unmercifully in his huge fists.

When the pair turned to face him with irritated looks, Thor smiled a wide, gap-toothed grin. He didn't raise his voice, but rather, spoke so softly that Irv and Hershel could barely hear his, "You are bothering my sister?"

When the men turned toward him, Thor raised himself to his full six-foot-six height and scowled. "My sister and her friend don't want be bothered, *forstå det*?"

It didn't matter that half of his sentence was in Norwegian, the two men quickly gathered up their drinks and moved to the far end of the bar. Thor strolled back to join his friends.

After a minute or two, the ladies came down to thank Thor. "I'm Cathy," the first lady, a full figured blond, told Thor holding out her hand. Thor blushed and laid a light kiss on the woman's hand. The second lady, a petite redhead, joined her and said, "Thank you so much. Those guys were really becoming a pain. I'm Sondra."

About that time, Ralph moved King Irv and company to a large table off to the side to wait for his friend. Sondra and Cathy joined them, sensing that they were gentlemen and not on the make. "You aren't from around here, are you?" Cathy asked which brought a chuckle from both Jules Verne and Hershel. King Irv kept a straight and dignified face.

"Have you ever been to France?" Verne asked them.

"Oh, you're visiting from France?" Sondra gushed.

"I am," Verne told them, "But my friends are traveling from elsewhere. May I present Irving and Hershel?" he told the ladies nodding toward the king and his Merlin.

"And the man who saved us from those two predators?" Cathy asked.

"That would be Thor," King Irv smiled. "He's from Norway. He doesn't know too much English, but he is a *true* gentleman."

"So we noticed," Sondra said giving Thor a wide smile.

King Irv asked if he could put the ladies drinks on his tab, "just as a friendly gesture," he assured them. The ladies giggled that they would be honored to be the guests of these worldly gentlemen.

Shortly before nine, some musicians began setting up in the back corner, across from the tap room. Ralph came by to tell King Irv that they had music for dancing scheduled. "If you'd like to be moved to a private room where it would be quieter to meet with Jerry?"

Irv, Hershel and Verne put their heads together for a quick confab and decided it would be beneficial to stay where they were. "Suit yourself," Ralph told them as he turned to go.

Around nine o'clock, Jerry arrived. He was dressed to the nines in a yellow zoot suit with two tone dancing shoes and a red bow tie. "Where's the women?" he panted.

Ralph introduced Jerry to Jules, King Irv, Thor and Hershel and then explained their problem. Jerry's eyes kept traveling to Sondra and Cathy, who had been briefed about the man Thor and company were planning to meet. Eventually Jerry became intrigued by the story Ralph was relaying. When Ralph proposed that they might "beam" a small group of hearty Vikings up to the barn on his father's farm for a few days, just until they could fix the time travel device on their Viking ship, Jerry got very excited.

"Vikings? You mean *real* Vikings, traveling across time?"

"Their ship is currently sitting in the bay disguised as a pleasure craft," Ralph told his friend. "If you can provide a place for them to hide, I'll send up a couple free kegs of ale to keep everyone happy until we can bring them back to their ship." "Why not?" Jerry agreed, "I love all that old Scandinavian history. And it sounds like it could be a fun party too. Maybe if I could let the word slip, some girls would come up there to join us." He tipped his head toward the secretaries accompanying King Irv's party.

When their business had been discussed, Jerry asked if Sondra and Cathy would like to dance. Sondra told him they had to be headed home soon as they had a long day of work tomorrow but Cathy smiled and said, "But a dance or two would be nice. Your friends have been so helpful to us."

When Irv, Hershel and Thor returned to the Motel 8, Jerry was still on the floor tripping the light fantastic with the two secretaries.

CHAPTER THIRTY

B ack at the Alameda County Jail, the Vikings were getting restless. They wanted their swords and hammers back and they wanted their freedom. Of all the lands they'd visited, no one had every treated them so rudely.

Granted, they'd been attacked by farmers bearing pitchforks, had boiling oil poured over them from castle walls, and had flaming arrows fired in their direction, but they'd never simply been rounded up and put behind bars when they'd had a few too many drinks. By the rules of engagement, if these people had a problem with them, they should stand up and face them with swords, or whatever other weapons they might possess. What kind of cowards would simply lock them behind steel doors and brick walls without a fair fight?

While the Englishman, Miles, counseled them to just be calm and wait for Thor or the English king to make some arrangement, Lars, Bolder and others cried out for action. If they could break the wooden bunks free of the chains that suspended those boards, they could use them as battering rams, knock down the walls and return to their ship. The vote of assembled prisoners was almost unanimous, with even some present day convicts from adjoining cells shouting to join in.

Rolf Andreson had been by a couple times to assure them he was doing all he could to win them their freedom. He even brought a young lady he knew, Kirsten, from the local Sons of Norway lodge, who spoke some Norwegian as an interpreter, but the Norse sailors hadn't been pacified. They couldn't understand any of the finer points of modern law and didn't care to hear it if they did.

One of the Vikings, Ragnar, who had spent some time in Iceland, talked about the Icelandic Thingvellir, which this modern court sounded similar to, but the others wouldn't hear about it. Miles told Rolf that he didn't have any idea how to control this Old Norse mob. "If you can't get us out of here soon," Miles told him, "you're going to have some sort of *Gotterdammerung* on your hands."

Being a fan of Richard Wagner, Rolf understood what Miles was saying. He ushered Kirsten toward the door of the lockup, vowing to ask for even more than double fees if he should ever have to visit the Alameda Detention Center again.

CHAPTER THIRTY-ONE

Under Lars leadership, the men had prised the bunks free of the walls and chains, pulled many of the chains loose from the bricks, and were busy assigning the assembled men tasks for their jail break. One of the other detainees in the cell had put a band-aid over the video camera up in the corner. It was 2:00 am and it was pretty well known that the deputy assigned the early morning hours tended to nap a little when things seemed quiet.

The Vikings and their friends were huddled together in the center of their cell, wooden bunks and iron links stacked close to hand, when a whooshing noise came over them and they found themselves stretched out in a deep pile of hay within the weathered wooden walls of a large barn.

The sailors fanned out in a four-square formation to explore these new surroundings. They discovered that the large double doors to the east were not locked, and opened onto a wide, star-lit meadow. Meanwhile, in the east end of their enclosure, they discovered four large metal enclosures in which something was bubbling. The breeze escaping from the airlock smelled like yeast and home brew. The Vikings held a quick pow-wow and decided that they would wait in this barn, either for whoever was making beer for them, or for the brew to be ready for consumption.

They had only to wait for a few short hours. Just after daylight Thor arrived, accompanied by Hershel and some crazy Frenchman, to reassure them that everything was okay and they would soon have their dragon-headed ship back. The assembled Viking troop all gave forth with a cheer, all except one man. That was when they discovered that, somehow, the Alameda County Sheriff's Deputy, who tended to nod off on the night shift while guarding the cells, had been caught up in Jules Verne's transponder and beamed up along with the Vikings and assorted inmates. The man had awoken from a brief cap-nap by strange banging and other noises coming from the cells and had just come to the door to see what was going on when he was caught up in Jules Verne's transponder ray. Unwittingly, he found himself accompanying the drunk tank inmates to this pastoral brewery setting.

Deputy Dickson was a fairly new recruit to the Alameda Sheriff's Department. Delbert Dickson had joined the Marines right out of high school and been sent on a pair of tours in the Middle East, one in Afghanistan and one in Iraq. Dickson had hated the Marines, but it least his tour had gotten him off his father's ranch in south Texas. He'd figured being a sheriff in California had to be better than being sent home and it was more money than he could ever make back in Texas.

And now he found himself surrounded by men in animal skins who seemed more fearless then any of his soldier buddies in the corps. At the first cross look from these Viking fellows, he stood and pledged his loyalty to their cause.

Thor addressed his men, sharing what he'd learned over the past few days from Hershel, the king and Ralph. He asked them to be patient while their ship was restored to them and could once again take them back to their own age, where they could explore, fight and conquer. Thor assured his crew that their stay in this pastoral California setting would not last long, and while it did, their hosts would provide plenty of ale and food, along with granting them free reign over the lands within the boundary fences of their host's estate.

"I'll be staying here with you off and on," he told his men, "until the king and his man have brought our longboat back to life as it should be and we can return to our voyage of exploration."

The Viking crew sent up a cheer as the firkins at the rear of the barn were tapped and the ale began to flow. Deputy Dickson, although he couldn't understand the ancient Norwegian language, cheered right along. "When in Rome," he told himself, and from where he was sitting this 'Rome' looked pretty good to him. He picked up a red plastic cup and joined the queue at the ale tap.

CHAPTER THIRTY-TWO

With the Viking chieftain reunited among his crew, Hershel and Jules Verne started back toward the city and their room at Motel Eight. Their drive back to Oakland was much more comfortable with just the two of them in the small Fiat, especially as they rolled the windows down and aired the pong of Thor's unwashed bearskins out of the tiny vehicle.

A few miles down the road, they stopped at the Edwards Vineyard Tasting Room to sample some wine. As Verne perused the list of sample tastes available, Hershel snuck off and put some coins in the old pay telephone by the establishment's rest rooms. He called Melissa to let her know he was in town, but only got her answering machine as she was at work. Disappointed, he left a message, asking her to call him at the Oakland Motel 8. "I'm staying in room 17," he told her. "I'll be in town for a few more days."

Verne was halfway through the sample taste menu when the Merlin returned to the bar. "Find something you like, Jules?" he asked the Frenchman.

"The reds are all excellent," Verne replied, smacking his lips. "Do you have a favorite?"

They decided to share a bottle of the Edwards Special Cabernet. The grape seemed to cement a new, stronger bond of friendship between the two men and Verne pledged to dedicate the next day to working with Hershel on repairing his time machine.

The trio got a good night's sleep, Verne moving into the room Hershel had been sharing with Thor, and King Irv returning to his own private suite. They all met up the next morning, just after sunrise, in the lounge where they enjoyed the free scrambled eggs, waffles and coffee set forth by the management. With their bellies full, Hershel and Verne got down to business.

"If you can drive me to where I've concealed my own time machine," Jules Verne told Hershel, "I'll show you what tools I have. If they look like they might be useful, we'll go to this disguised boat of yours and set to work on your own time contrivance."

"Sure, alright," Hershel told him, "except there's cops all over Thor's boat. We're gonna just stroll right down the dock past them and tip our hats?"

"*Hershel*," the Frenchman laughed, "are we not both men of magic? Together, I'm sure we can conger up something to distract these modern lookouts."

"If you say so," Hershel replied skeptically.

The Frenchman directed Hershel through the streets of Berkeley and onto the University of California campus. They drove across the wide grounds to an area beyond the school's athletic fields. Just past the football stadium, Jules Verne directed Hershel to the top level of a deserted parking garage. In the farthest corner from the ramp sat what looked like a futuristic, though miniature, diesel railroad locomotive. Hershel pulled the yellow Fiat up beside the train-like vehicle and Verne jumped out of the car, waving a short metal wand over the contraption.

A hatch opened in the rear of the thing and Verne leaned in, coming back out with a stout leather satchel. He laid it on the ground beside the Fiat, undid two heavy metal fasteners and un-folded the lid. Small pockets within held various metal wrenches, rulers, calipers and screwdrivers.

"I can't say for sure, as I've never laid eyes on your device," Verne told Hershel, "but I should have everything we need right here."

Hershel made a face. "I don't see *anything* like what I need to get into my machine," he scoffed. "The calipers might come in handy for some measurements, or one of those screwdriver things, but I can't be sure. Maybe you need to come with me and check out how my machine works and then we can go shopping for the right gear to fix it."

"Shouldn't we at least bring my tool kit with us?" the French-man argued. "If something I have works, we could save valuable time."

"Yeah, sure," Hershel told him, "by all means. So let's think about what kinda magic spell we need while we head over to the marina."

The Frenchman had a very different approach to conjuring spells then Hershel, so it took some time to come to a common un-derstanding of how they each worked. It turned out to be more a question of language and semantics then physical deceptions and they finally came to an agreement on how to approach the problem.

After hours of driving around the city discussing what words and gestures would be used, they left the rented Fiat in the Ala-meda Marina parking area, a couple rows back from the seawall. Verne started to haul his leather case out of the car, but Hershel held out his palms in a "hold it right there" gesture. "Don't you think we should take a look at things before we start lugging a bag of tools around this place? We already look kinda suspicious as it is."

Verne nodded his head and pushed the satchel back behind the seats of the small yellow vehicle. He then stood up, straightened a black beret on his head and followed Hershel to the dockside and down the thin wooden wharf. About halfway down the pier, the Merlin removed a red-pink crystal from the back pocket of his jeans and began mumbling soft words the Frenchman couldn't quite make out. Verne cocked his head sideways to hear better, then realized that Hershel was speaking ancient Hebrew.

For just a flash, the second yacht down from the bay end of the pier turned into a dragon headed Viking ship, then just as quickly returned to the modern pleasure craft it was cloaked to look like, except that the uniformed deputy sitting with his arms folded across his chest seemed to stiffen and freeze mid-blink.

Hershel gave Jules Verne a 'thumbs-up' and a casual wink. The pair sped up their steps to the boat. The craft rocked slightly to and fro as they stepped aboard. The catatonic sheriff's deputy didn't move. Verne waved a hand in front of the policeman's face then let out a surprised sound when the man gave no sign of recognition.

Verne followed the Merlin to the center of the main deck, where Hershel stopped, scratched his head, and said, "So where in the heck did my time travel box get off to?" He held up his pink crystal and mumbled some more Hebrew.

The Yacht once more took its true appearance as an old longboat, remaining uncloaked for some twenty seconds until Hershel chuckled, "Oh, I get it now."

The Merlin led the way aft along the teak deck to a narrow door that would put them into the boat's main salon. Inside, the Merlin stood before a bank of cabinets, did a sort of 'einie, mee-nie, miney, moe,' gesture and pulled open the center cupboard door. Inside the compact space sat the broken box holding Her-shel's invention.

"Drag a chair over here, Jules," he stated without looking around at his partner. Verne pulled a heavy stool on a wide metal base over to Hershel and started to sit. Hershel stopped him with a look, then waved the Frenchman over beside himself.

"Let's pull this box out and set in on the chair. We'll have bet-ter light that way and we can look the whole contraption over with-out poking our heads into this hole in the wall."

Hershel showed the Frenchman where the knob had broken off, explaining that he didn't know how they could set destinations through time or space with the stem of the controls broken off so deep inside.

"I sealed this thing too damn well," he mumbled under his breath. "I got a response one time when I jammed a seashell into the hole, but that ain't the answer."

"What's that?" Verne inquired.

"Nothing," Hershel replied, "Only I'm afraid I might have to cut the thing in half to get at the gear the knob is supposed to turn. Any suggestions?"

Jules Verne put two fingers under his beret and scratched at his scalp. "My own time machine doesn't have knobs," he told Her-shel. "It's controlled by a sort of 'cats whisker' needle which runs along a board swathed in coils of copper. I don't suppose that's what's inside this box of yours?"

"Cats whiskers and copper," Hershel laughed. "I've never heard of such a thing. My machine is full of crystals of fine white quartz. Do you know how expensive copper is? Or how hard it is to find in the area around Irv's kingdom?"

CHAPTER THIRTY-THREE

Word of the weird jailbreak spread rapidly even as the Sheriff's Department tried to keep it under wraps. Sheriff Benson had no idea where to start looking for prisoners who simply vanished into thin air. He had no getaway vehicle, no trail to follow, no clues to research; in a phrase, he had bump-kiss, zip.

Sheriff Benson was also extremely worried about his young rookie deputy, Delbert Dickson. He considered this to be a hostage situation even though no one had contacted him to say they were holding the man prisoner. All he knew was that they'd taken his young Deputy with them.

Darlene Shacly, meanwhile, was scheduled to be released from custody in spite of the fact that she was being totally un-cooperative. She would tell the deputies nothing other than the fact that she was totally head-over-heels in love with one of these weird Viking creatures. Sheriff Benson figured he'd let Stan Shacly deal with his crazy daughter.

Darlene wasn't above borrowing one of daddy's credit cards when she wanted something. She felt entitled as she was given such a small weekly allowance beyond the money for her school books and tuition. Right now, she needed lots of funding to locate her new life's love. She didn't care what her parents might try to do to her somewhere down the line, right now she wanted to be with Bjorn, no matter what it might cost her.

She remembered that while she was incarcerated in that motel room cell, the jail matron, a Hispanic lady named Anna Marie, had talked on endlessly about her daughter who would be turning eighteen in a few weeks. Anna Marie was very upset that she didn't have enough money to buy her daughter the new car the girl wanted. Hell, she didn't even have enough to make the down payment on a new car, which she would gladly do, co-signing for her daughter if it would make the girl happy, anything for her favorite little girl.

Darlene had a plan formulating in her pretty little head. She telephoned the county center and asked for Anna Marie in the county jail section. The desk sergeant wouldn't put her call through, but offered to leave a message for the jailer.

"Tell her I was concerned about her daughter's birthday and wanted to help out if I could," Darlene told the woman, then left her cell phone number without giving her name.

Anna Marie rang back in less than half an hour. "You can help me?" she inquired hopefully. "And who is this?"

"It's me, Darlene," Shacly's daughter answered. "I was so moved by your dilemma when you were guarding me in that motel room that I went right to my father, you know who my father is, right? I went right to daddy and asked if we couldn't somehow help you get a car for your daughter."

"Oh, Holy Mother in Heaven," Anna Marie shouted back. "I prayed that someone would help me. Oh, bless you, Miss Shacly. I'll do anything for you. You name it, anything."

"Well, there is one little thing," Darlene replied coyly, "but I'd rather not discuss it over the telephone. Could we meet later, after you get off work? I'll buy you a drink. Where could we get together?"

"Oh, thank you, Miss Shacly. I don't drink... Could we maybe meet at Saint Mary Magdalene Church on Berryman Street? I'll wait for you in the main cathedral at five o'clock this evening."

"Whatever," Darlene replied. She wasn't much of a church-goer, but this was important business. "See you there."

Darlene was waiting among the dark pews when Anna Marie entered the main hall of the church. She stood and signaled. She was tempted to put two fingers in her mouth and whistle, but figured that the women would notice her without such a rude noise. This was, after all, the House of God, at least in some people's minds.

"And what kind of car is your daughter hoping to have?" Darlene asked in greeting the woman.

"Oh, I think she would be happy with anything nice and clean," the lady jailer replied. "Just so it is reliable."

Darlene breathed an inward sigh of relief. At least the woman wouldn't be expecting a BMW or Mercedes.

"I can get a good, late model car for you," Darlene stated confidently. She would be willing to give up her own vehicle if it would put her in the arms of Bjorn, her Viking lover.

"But first, I must ask a small favor of you. Do you have access to the sheriff's department computers?"

"Oh no," Anna Marie cried with a worried expression. "I mean, yes, I have a password so that I can enter data into these computers, but..."

"I don't want to get you in any trouble," Darlene told the jailer. "I only want to find the cell phone number of this deputy sheriff who was taken hostage, what is his name, Dickson? If I can help to locate him, then I can prove that I'm not some kind of criminal, do you understand?"

Anna Marie's face brightened at this. "Yes, yes! I'm most willing to help you… And my Lupe will get her motor car for her birthday, yes?"

"Yes," Darlene assured. "So first, I want you to get me Deputy Dickson's personal cell phone number…"

"Yes, I can do this…"

"And then I can try to call him and make sure that he's okay." Darlene grinned.

CHAPTER THIRTY-FOUR

As quickly as Anna Marie telephoned her with Delbert Dickson's cell phone information, Darlene was on the phone to a former boyfriend, who she knew was still interested in her and who was a computer science major at Berkeley.

"Bertie," she grinned into the phone. "I need one huge favor from you and then maybe we can get together next Saturday for that big beer bust out in Walnut Creek. I've just really been missing you so much!"

"Darlene?" came the reply. "Is this really Darlene? I thought you said you didn't want anything to do with me as I was such a complete and utter nerd?"

"Oh, Bertie," she giggled, "You know I have my moods… Now I have this cell phone number. I want you to do that 'triangulate' thing with it and see if you can find where it's at right now."

"Is this some other guy who dumped you who you're trying to find?" he asked suspiciously.

"Oh, Bertie, you are so dramatic," she wailed. "It's just some client of fathers who skipped out. If I can find him for daddy, I might get an increase in my allowance… Then *I* can take *you* out for a big dinner next week."

Bertie sounded a bit skeptical, but his lust for Darlene's charms, not to mention her father's money, won out. "Oh, all right. Give me the number and I'll get back to you before happy hour starts at the

Metaphysical Brewing Company. Meet me there and I'll let you know what I find out."

Darlene didn't really want to be stuck chatting with Bertie the Nerd for an hour or more, but it might be the only way she could locate Bjorn. She would just have to steel herself and endure what was necessary. Bertram Pearce was such an uncool freak!

Bertie was waiting at the Metaphysical Brewing Company when Darlene walked in. The shine in his eyes told her that he'd started imbibing without her. The confident square of his shoulders told her that he definitely had something good for her.

"Can I buy your next one, Bertie?" she asked, sliding onto the empty bar stool next to him. "Maybe, after a few rounds, we could go somewhere more intimate?"

She could see the young man's excitement rising. His breathing was accelerating and small beads of sweat were breaking out on his forehead.

"But don't you want to know about that cell phone?" he cried, "to make your father happy and get you a bigger allowance?"

"Oh, Bertie," she giggled, "I already *knew* you'd have that for me. I have great confidence in you."

Young Bertram pulled his cell phone from his pocket and waved it before Darlene's face. "Here it is," he blurbed excitedly. "This is the location your father needs to check out."

Darlene took Bertie's phone from his hand, placed it on the bar, and then brought a legal pad from her large straw purse, which she set next to the phone. As their drinks arrived, she quickly made notes from the young man's i-Pad. When she had all the information she needed, Darlene stood up quickly, slapped her forehead and declared, "Oh my God. I forgot to put money in the parking meter!" as she bolted from the bar, exiting through the rear.

Bertie took another pull from his ale, waiting patiently, when it suddenly dawned on him. If Darlene was parked out in the back lot, there wouldn't *be* any parking meters. The Metaphysical Brewing Company provided oodles of free parking just outside their back door.

The duped young man let out a cry and stood, heading for the exit, but was stopped by the pub's very large bouncer, Klaus.

"Were you not planning to pay for the drinks you and the lady ordered?" Klaus inquired.

"The lady was on her own," Bertie shouted indignantly.

"But she was with *you*, sir," Klaus smiled, "And she's already gone, leaving you responsible, sir. Are you denying that you were with the lady?"

"Erm, well, I mean I was kinda talking with her, but I never offered to buy her a drink…"

"But she is gone now, sir," Klaus reasoned. "So I believe you are, as we say, stuck with buying her a drink. I only hope you have a phone number or something. Maybe you can get the lady to reimburse you?"

Bertie tossed a wad of bills at the large man and with a dirty look, stormed out the door to his car.

CHAPTER THIRTY-FIVE

Hershel and Jules drove all over the San Francisco Bay area. They checked out electronics wholesalers, discount dealers and dollar stores without finding much of what the Merlin could recognize as being useful to get his time travel thingy back on line. Hershel did buy a cheap set of calipers and some long, narrow screwdrivers with flat blades.

At a jewelry store along the way, Verne urged Hershel to buy a jeweler's loupe.

"What is that?" the Merlin asked in a quizzical tone. The salesman demonstrated, helping Hershel screw it up to his eye and check out the workings of an old pocket watch.

"Oh yeah," Hershel told his French friend, "I can see where this could come in handy."

The two men returned to the Motel 8 for a mid afternoon nap after all their rushing around. They found King Irv pacing the floor of his room.

"This is all just becoming too much," the monarch told them. "I need to get back to Warehouse Castle to make sure everything is alright with my kingdom."

"Majesty," Hershel hollered, "I'm still trying to get the stuff I need to fix my time machine. I don't know what more I can do to help. I'm really sorry, highness. I'm doing all I can, and this Verne guy is doing what he can to help as well."

In an instant, King Irv's continence brightened. "Mr. Verne, do you not also have a time machine... A *working* time machine?"

Jules Verne gave a slight bow. "You know I do, your highness, but..."

"How would you like to visit a traditional Hebrew kingdom in very early England? I'll bet you could get a book or two out of such an experience."

"But I am mostly interested in writing about *futuristic* situations, your highness," Verne replied. "What we call Science Fiction; fantastic stories about ships that fly through space and boats that travel under the ocean, and things like that..."

"But such knowledge of ancient times could be beneficial to your thinking, if not your writing," King Irv pressed, "is this not so?"

"Well," Verne hesitated.

"Well there you have it," King Irv told him. "While we wait for a solution to these Viking prisoners and Hershel fixing his time machine, why don't you accompany me back to my home in the Wholesale Kingdom? I can teach you to play golf and you can meet my family. You can even sample pizza, a dish my daughter pinched from the future. Have you ever had pizza?"

Jules Verne shook his head, a bit dazed by King Irv's rapid-fire monologue. "I don't know what to say," he uttered. "I've seen pizza advertised around the city here..."

"And you were curious, weren't you," his Highness pushed. "Well we've got the *original*, not some modern knock-off pizza recipe." Hershel rolled his eyes behind Jules Verne's back.

"I'm not sure I understand? What has pizza got to do with writing novels? What are you talking about?"

"Then it's settled," King Irv chortled. "Let's get over to this time travel thing of yours and head for old England!"

Up to the north of San Francisco Bay, things were going a little sideways. Darlene Shacly, who had managed to get a fix on Deputy Dickson's personal cell phone, arrived at the secluded farm where the Vikings were sequestered, driving a V-10 Audi R-8 roadster that she'd borrowed from her father's rare car collection. To her, it was just another car, the closest to the barn door, albeit it was a very pretty machine, gun metal blue with a sleek black leather top. She lowered the top and backed the roadster out of the car barn then headed north over the Golden Gate Bridge. She had a little trouble with the six-on-the-floor transmission, and tended to grind the gears a bit, but she was able to get the machine out on the highway.

The Audi was the real estate mogul's newest acquisition and his most prized motor, sure to be missed if Stan Shacly had been paying attention, but he was currently out of town on a mission to Havana, Cuba, where he was stocking up on exotic cigars he could use to bribe city officials before the Oakland council was to vote on new real estate tax increases.

Arriving at the location Bertie had provided, Darlene flew from her borrowed roadster and burst into a barn-like structure at the back of the property shouting for Bjorn, but Bjorn was passed out down by a stream that ran at the edge of the property. Bjorn had consumed more than his share from the kegs that the Metaphysical Brewing Company had provided, and had gone in search of a place to rest his head.

As none of the Vikings spoke much English, no one could understand what this crazy woman from the frightful blue machine was on about. They knew the word bjorn, which meant 'bear,' but they didn't connect it with their drunken friend. No one saw any bear in the area to threaten them, but it was better to be safe than sorry. The bearded rabble took up pitchforks and sticks to defend this poor young woman against the bear she was shouting about, and they spread out around the property looking for the animal, but to no avail. Miles wasn't available to translate this woman's babbling for them as he had staggered down by the stream, very drunk, with his pal Bjorn.

Darlene followed them, confused by their actions. Were they set to harm her lover with their sticks and farm implements? Maybe they were jealous of her lover's good fortune in having her as a girlfriend? "Stop," she shouted. "Don't you dare harm my lover."

The Vikings looked around in confusion. Was there a bear or not? What was this woman saying? Their bewildered stumbling and shouting managed to bring the Viking sailor, Bjorn, out of his stupor. He staggered up the rise from the slim trickle of water where he had lain, angry about being awoken from his troubled sleep. When he saw his shipmates approaching with their weapons, Bjorn let loose with an angry roar.

Then he saw Darlene. Actually, he saw two Darlenes in his drunken state, and his inebriated face broke into a happy grin. He lurched forward to give her a hug, but missed his girl and fell face down into a pile of rotting leaves.

Darlene dropped down beside her Viking lover, wrapped her arms around him and gave him a deep soulful kiss. Bjorn pulled his mouth back from Darlene's and threw up all over her, then gave her a sloppy but pleased grin, and passed out again at her feet mumbling, "jeg elske." 'I love you' in old Norse .

Bird the Cat looked on in amusement from the low branch of a nearby pine tree.

CHAPTER THIRTY-SIX

King Irv had dragged Verne and Hershel down to the Metaphysical Brewing Company where he continued his badgering of the Frenchman about taking him back to England, like in his time machine. In a moment of weakness, and after several pints, Verne admitted that he *was* curious about such a kingdom as Irv was describing. King Irv immediately threw an arm over Hershel's shoulder and asked if he couldn't please drive them over to Verne's time travel thing before the evening got too late.

"Drive you to Jules' contraption?" Hershel spat back, "Like, you mean right now? You could see it much better in the daylight, your highness."

"Tonight," Irv thundered. "I don't just wish to see it, I wish to ride in it back to Warehouse Castle." Then, in a whisper, he added, "Quick, before this man changes his mind!"

Hershel shifted his eyes rapidly between Verne and his monarch. "Well, sure, Irv, I mean that would be fine...But why?"

"Hershel," the king continued, whispering with wide eyes, "I've been away for too long. I must take some time out and see that my kingdom is running as it should. I cannot wait on you, much as I love you, to get your time machine back in order. My queen and my subjects may be in dire need of me right now. It is my solemn and sworn duty to see to my affairs of state." Then, in a normal voice, he told his Merlin, "Monsieur Verne and I will return in a week or two. Hopefully, by then, you will have your time machine sorted out.

"If not, well, we may have to look at other options, whatever they might be, I cannot say. You've always been a good friend and a faithful servant, Hershel, but I *do* have a kingdom to run, do you understand?"

Hershel's face was crestfallen. "Highness?" he pleaded.

"I'm sorry, Hershel. Let us pray that you will find some answers for your contraption before I return. I don't know what else I can do. I'll ask the Rabbi to pray for you when I get home."

Turning to Jules Verne with a wide grin, Irv said, "You won't be sorry, my friend. I know you're going to love the Wholesale Kingdom. It'll be a great and relaxing holiday for you, mark my words, just what you need to get the old creative juices flowing."

The Frenchman just sat there gob struck.

In the multi-level parking structure near the University of California athletic fields, King Irv stepped out of Hershel's rented Fiat. He pulled the handle that released the seat forward and let Jules Verne exit from the rear compartment of the vehicle. Verne withdrew a small valise from the sub-compact car. King Irv needed nothing more than the clothes on his back.

Jules Verne waved his wand over the streamlined train looking thing that sat in the lot, watched the doors open and then helped King Irv inside. As Hershel looked on, the futuristic vehicle began to shimmer and fade.

Hershel let forth a deep sigh as his monarch and best friend disappeared from sight along with the strange Frenchman who they had only encountered a few days before.

When the top level of the parking structure was empty, Hershel turned his tiny yellow car around and headed back for the Motel 8, near the brewery in Oakland. He brightened up on the drive back, thinking that now at least he'd be able to spend some time with Melissa up in Napa. Before the Fiat crossed from Berkeley back into Oakland, Hershel was smiling and humming an off-key tune.

Later, at the brewery bar, Ralph inquired after King Irv when Hershel returned. "He had to go back to old England," the Merlin replied with sad eyes. "He went back and didn't even offer to take me."

"Smart man, I'd say," Ralph told Hershel with a wink. "He doesn't want to be around here when the you-know-what hits the fan with all those crazy Vikings up at the farm. Too bad he's left you holding the can."

"Holding the can?" Hershel echoed.

"It's an expression," Ralph told him. "It means... oh, heck, it means he's left you to answer for things, I'm sorry."

"My king wouldn't do that to me," Hershel cried indignantly, "Would he?"

Ralph excused himself to check on a couple down at the far end of the bar. Hershel put some notes on the bar and returned to his lonely room at the Motel 8.

Nothing on modern television could hold his interest and Melissa still wasn't answering her telephone. Hershel's mind kept flowing over his broken time machine, the current crazy situation with these Viking people and his King being far off in time at their castle. With nothing further to interest him, Hershel went down, started up the Fiat and headed out to the Alameda Marina to have another go at his time machine.

CHAPTER THIRTY-SEVEN

Queen Sophie became excited when she saw something silvery shimmering into view near the Merlin's cave, just off the first fairway of King Irv's golf course. She didn't know what to think when the object solidified into a thing more like one of the railroad trains she'd seen on her visits to modern England, but she was very happy when King Irv stepped forth holding his arms out to her.

Irv and Sophie embraced, then kissed. When their faces disconnected, Irv introduced her to Monsieur Jules Verne, explaining how the Frenchman from the future had been able to transport him home when Hershel's machine had failed. Sophie thanked Verne profusely, asking if he would be staying on as their guest.

"Of course he'll be staying with us," King Irv scolded. "He brought me back, he knows no one else here and we are in his debt for helping me."

Queen Sophie grinned and curtsied to the Frenchman. "Welcome to Warehouse Castle," she cooed. "I'm so glad you could join us, and thank you for returning my husband to me."

King Irv guided Verne on a tour of his small kingdom as the sun was setting, introducing him to his son, Prince Sol, and Debbie at the Pizza and Wine Café, where they stopped to see the kingdom's tame dragon, Smokey. The small dancing dragon brought a grin to the Frenchman's usually serious face. "I've never seen anything quite like this," he told his hosts.

When they returned to Warehouse Castle, Sophie showed the Frenchman to a suite of rooms on the castle's second floor. The servants prepared a light supper served with Cabernet wine for the King's guest and then they all retired for the night.

The next morning, King Irv was up early, planning the day. He wanted to introduce Verne to his golf course and maybe teach him the game. If and when they might try out the game of golf, Irv had a six-pack or two of tinned ale from the future to impress his guest.

But Verne wasn't at all interested in either golf or tinned ale. By late afternoon, seated in the main room of Warehouse Castle, Queen Sophie suggested that they imbibe some more of her special Cabernet wine. She had a servant bring forth a tray with a bottle, some stemmed glasses and a cork screw.

Jules Verne's eyes lit up at the sight of a wine bottle and stemmed glasses. "This is more like it," he beamed. "It's that wine we had last night, isn't it? It tastes very much like a vintage Hershel introduced me to when we went up to see those crazy Viking fellows north of San Francisco. A Frenchman is always ready to enjoy a good wine."

While King Irv slurped his ale, Queen Sophie and the Frenchman polished off three bottles of the kingdom's special red wine before the kitchen served them dinner. Prince Sol, who always enjoyed his mother's special wine, seemed to be forming a solid friendship with Monsieur Verne. By the end of the night, they had all formed a unique bond. Jules Verne told them he'd never had such an enjoyable evening as he rose to retire to his rooms.

On the following day, a Thursday, King Irv had horses saddled for himself and his guest. After a breakfast of bagels with cream cheese, they set out across the Wholesale Kingdom for the North

Sea. Irv pointed out to Verne where the Vikings had appeared, and both men dismounted to walk along the sandy shoreline. But there were no longboats in the harbor on this day.

The two saddled up again and rode northwest to the Kingdom of Vaude, where Irv introduced his guest to his son's brother-in-law, King John. As they visited, the Frenchman wrote notes in a small pad he carried on his person. When King John gave Verne a quizzical look, the Frenchman told him that he was always gathering useful information.

"I write books," Verne replied solemnly. "I may not be writing about your particular time, but everything I see is likely to jar ideas for the scenes I create in my mind. I hope you don't mind?"

King John gave a puzzled look toward King Irv, then when the monarch of Wholesale Castle grinned back at him, he said, "By all means, write on. I'm sure it can do no harm."

Irv leaned close to his son-in-law and whispered, "Nothing Rutherford or Judith have told me indicates that, in the present, any of this man's writings are about us. It's all something they call Science Fiction."

"I'm currently working on a book about a boat that travels under the sea," Verne grinned. "I call it a submarine, a vessel I am christening The Nautilus. That's why I happened to be in San Francisco. In my book, I planned to have sailors from San Francisco terrified of this underwater boat... Only I arrived in San Francisco a bit late for the time in which I wanted to set my book."

On the ride back to Warehouse Castle, King Irv asked, "Are you sure you wouldn't like to learn something about our game called golf?"

"Quite sure," Verne replied. "But I would be most curious to take a look in your Merlin, Hershel's, cave, if that could be permitted."

"Well, I don't know..." Irv began.

"I'm not looking to steal any of your man's ideas or inventions," Verne assured the monarch. "I promise not to take anything away with me beyond my written notes, you may accompany me to see that I hold true to my word. I'm only curious about the man's methods, his findings being so far advanced for what we, in my time, think of as such a primitive period of history as yours."

CHAPTER THIRTY-EIGHT

Back in the future, Hershel returned to the Motel 8 in the early hours to find that Melissa had called him twice. She left a message that she had been in a meeting all day and then had gone out with the girls for a drink afterwards. She was very sorry that she'd missed Hershel's calls and hoped that they could get together soon. "Call me after five tomorrow evening," her message said. "I'd really like to see you again."

So all day Friday, the Merlin moped around, unsure what to do with himself. He went back to bed for an hour or so, then drove back down to the marina where he snuck aboard the pseudo-yacht and stared at his time machine for another hour. No giant revelation came to him about how to make the thing work again even though he turned it every-which-way on the chair and approached it from all angles. He even set it on end and stared down the shaft of the broken knob with his new jeweler's loupe, but to no avail.

Late afternoon found Hershel back in the Metaphysical Brewery seated in front of a pint of ale and a hamburger. As he spread ketchup over his French fried potatoes he thought about what to say to Melissa when he finally connected with her. Melissa believed that he was a traveling salesman from England supplying exotic wine making equipment to the growers of the California wine country.

Was it time to tell her his real story? Would she even believe such a tale? And how would it affect their relationship? I mean, he didn't want to marry the woman or anything like that, but he *did* enjoy her company when he was so far away from home in time and space.

As he tipped the last drop of ale over his lips, the Merlin decided he'd leave things just as they were. He'd like to get her opinion on what to do about all those Viking fellows in the barn and his being temporarily stuck here in the future, but was that worth risking all the fun he had with this modern woman who accepted him as just another man from her own time?

Hershel walked back to the pay phone in the back hall and went to drop some coins into the slot, but the slot was gone. In its place was a row of tiny flashing red lights over a small grooved track. The lights would intermittently blink in various patterns, then would spell out letters that moved along the screen telling him to just 'swipe his credit card' and direct dial his number.

"What the hell," he mumbled. Irv had the credit card, he thought. The he remembered that he had a spare somewhere in his bag back at the motel. Hershel left the handset swinging free beneath the wall-mounted call box, went back out to throw some dollar bills on the bar, and then walked back up the avenue to the Motel 8.

Once in his room, the Merlin realized he didn't need to look for his card or go back to the brewery to make his call. He could dial a number nine, then Melissa's number and they'd just put the call on his room bill. He reclined back on the big double bed, picked up the receiver and dialed Melissa's number from memory.

His lady friend picked up on the first ring. "Hershel? Oh, how I've missed you. These American men are just... Well, they just aren't as suave, or, ah, as interesting as you Englishmen. So how are you?"

"I'm much better now, hearing your voice," the Merlin gushed, "So how've you been?"

CHAPTER THIRTY-NINE

Hershel made a date to pick Melissa up in two hours. She mentioned an English pub and restaurant called the Pelican, out near the coast. "They've got that ale stuff you like on draught there," she told him. "So you don't have to drink wine. You pretend to love wine, but I can tell you'd rather be drinking ale," she giggled, "and I want you to be happy, Hershel, very happy."

The Merlin grinned inwardly. This lady wanted him to be happy, and he knew that she could make him very, very happy. Hershel couldn't wait to see this crazy American lady who wanted to make him happy. He pushed the Fiat close to the speed limit all the way up Interstate Highway 80 to Napa, where Melissa lived in a small apartment near the center of the town.

His lady was dressed in tight-fitting jeans and a low cut blouse with a comic cat print all over it in black and grey. The tails of her top were tied in a knot over her navel and her cleavage beckoned like the Grand Canyon as she answered the door with a clinging hug and a deep soul kiss.

This might have been a warning to a more attuned man but Hershel could only think of the pleasure this woman was about to lay on him. He returned her kiss tongue-for-tongue then led her down the steps to his rented Fiat where he held her door open for her, then walked around to put himself behind the wheel.

Melissa directed Hershel over the two-lane country roads toward the coast and the little inn where they would dine. True to her word, it looked just like an old English public house, a white building with green trim perched on a small rise just off the beach. Hershel thought that maybe he'd been here before, but he wasn't sure.

"I called ahead and made us reservations," she told the Merlin. "We have a table back in the corner where no one can disturb us." More red warning flags flew right over Hershel's head.

As soon as they were seated, a pint glass of amber ale was set before Hershel along with an uncorked bottle of red wine and a glass for his lady. A second waiter brought menus in black leather covers. "Give us a few minutes," Melissa smiled up at the man.

Hershel was into his second pint of the strong ale before the waiter returned. Melissa ordered for both of them.

"We'll have the local, fresh-caught lobster," she told the man, "with new potatoes and green beans."

The waiter mumbled, "Very good, madam," and seemed to shimmer away toward the kitchen.

Hershel, already sporting a strong buzz, just grinned and nodded his head in the affirmative. Melissa grabbed his hand under the table and placed it on her knee, giving him a wicked grin which screamed, "Yes, you may."

Their dinner was like a scene from that English film with Alfie Finney about Tom Jones. They grinned and leered at each other while they ate and drank. Hershel lost count of how many ales he'd consumed before the wait staff brought the raspberry trifles. Melissa drove them back to Napa where she tucked Hershel into her bed winking at herself in the mirror over her vanity.

When the sun came through the window of Melissa's apartment to kiss the red and raw eyes of Hershel the Merlin, he was alone under the black and white pop-art Ikea spread of the girl's full size bed, but he could smell coffee nearby. The Merlin smiled inwardly although for the life of him he couldn't remember just what he'd done the night before. He was sure, however, that it had been a memorable experience and that he'd enjoyed it thoroughly. It would come to him eventually when he thought back.

Melissa entered the room carrying one of those trays with little fold-down legs, which she placed on the bed over Hershel, telling him to sit up straight. The Merlin did as instructed and saw before him a plate overflowing with fried eggs, bacon and buttered toast. Hershel reached out a hand and pushed the bacon off to one side, bacon not something his religious training would allow him to eat.

"Melissa, baby, you shouldn't have," he murmured as he brought his other arm from beneath the covers and rubbed his hands together. Melissa poured two cups of coffee, set them on the tray and carefully climbed into the bed beside him.

Taking a sip of her coffee, she looked deep into his eyes and asked, "Hershel, do you really love me?"

Hershel nodded in the affirmative, his mouth full of eggs and toast. He swallowed and then added, "Oh yeah, sure baby. Oh yeah, I really love you."

"Really, really love me?" Melissa asked again, her eyes still boring deep into his own.

"Sure, course I do," Hershel assured her, taking another swallow of the hot and excellent coffee.

"Enough to marry me and take me back to England with you?" the girl purred, then with a quizzical look she added, "You're not already married, are you?"

Hershel choked on his coffee, spraying some of the hot brown liquid across Melissa's fresh, clean bedspread. After a few choking breaths he assured her that he wasn't married, but the girl wasn't really listening.

"Only, I've just been given notice at my job yesterday," she went on, "and I don't know where else I can get a good job around here… And I'm kinda fed up with America right now anyway. Our current President is really loony.

"After we're married maybe I could be your secretary or some-thing?" she mused with a dreamy look.

CHAPTER FORTY

Right through the Sabbath and into the next week, Jules Verne spent his days combing through Hershel's cave, reading all the Merlin's notes and copying Hershel's various equations into his little pad of papers.

At first, King Irv hung close to the Frenchman, sipping ale and eyeing his every move. But by sundown on the Sabbath, this was becoming quite boring. Irv excused himself for the Holy day and left the Frenchman at his word that he would take nothing.

When Irv returned Sunday morning, Verne was still busy scribbling notes. He had, by now, borrowed sheaves of Hershel's own blank parchments to keep his notes going.

"I'll be glad to pay you for the paper I'm using, if that's an issue," he told Irv.

"No," Irv mumbled. "Don't worry about it, only, don't you think it's time we were getting back to join Hershel and the Vikings?"

"I'm almost through with my research here," Verne told him, without looking the monarch in the eye, "Maybe by late tomorrow or the day after?"

King Irv scowled, but the Frenchman didn't look around to catch the monarch's unhappy face. "I do have a kingdom to run here," Irv thundered.

"And I hope I'm not getting in your way," Verne replied, still without looking around. "Just go and do what you have to do. I'll be finished as soon as I can…"

"You'll be finished by mid day tomorrow," King Irv thundered, "Or sooner. And as soon as you are, you will bring me back to the Metaphysical Brewing Company in San Francisco to reunite with my friends. Do you understand me? It would be a shame if you were not able to leave this time, and could never write these books you are planning!"

Jules Verne looked up in surprise.

"I do have a stable of knights to enforce my wishes," Irv told him, pinning the Frenchman with dark eyes. "And my son-in-law in the next kingdom has more such knights if it should come to that."

"We shall be ready to leave shortly after breakfast tomorrow," the Frenchman replied curtly.

True to his word, Jules Verne had his bag packed the next morning and was waiting patiently beside his time machine when King Irv came out from breakfast.

Jules Verne hit his controls and they materialized in the parking lot behind the Metaphysical Brewery right around sunset. The Happy Hour crowd parked BMWs, Lincolns and Audis all around Verne's old diesel train looking thing, giving him high fives and admiring looks. Bay Area people loved anything unique.

Inside the brew pub, Ralph told Irv that Hershel was probably up in Marin County, keeping an eye on Thor and his crazy Vikings. Their rooms were still reserved at the Motel 8 up the street, but it didn't look like anyone had been staying there for a few days.

Verne's immediate reaction was that they should get right back in his time machine and set the dials for this farm where the Vikings were stationed. But King Irv's cooler head prevailed. They would pop down the street to the Motel 8, leaving Jules Verne's contraption behind the brewery, sleep on things, and then discuss what their next move should be over the free breakfast in the morning. Verne, who wasn't so sure that what the Motel 8 served actually constituted real breakfast, argued against such a move.

"Breakfast?" he shouted. "You call American waffles and fried eggs breakfast? Without croissants or yogurt? No fresh figs?"

"Okay," Irv conceded. "So we'll have coffee and talk about what to do next, alright? Jeez, I hate semantics!"

CHAPTER FORTY-ONE

King Irv slept well and woke up later than he had intended. A new habit acquired living in this future land, he fingered the remote button beside his bed and turned on that big picture window thing on the wall across from his bed, then went to start the machine that provided the future drink, coffee, that he'd become so fond of. When he turned back to the television thing in his room, he almost spit the coffee all over himself, having trouble holding the ceramic Motel 8 mug steady.

On the screen, police in khaki uniforms were exiting military-looking vehicles to surround some kind of farm. It was, in fact, the very farm where Thor and his Vikings had hidden themselves. Irv recognized it by the surroundings. The uniformed men all brandished nasty looking modern guns. None of them looked happy, wearing grim visages as they looked out over the valley where Thor's men hid.

Leaving his room, Irv ran to the room where he assumed Hershel, his Merlin was staying, but the room was empty, the bed unslept in.

King Irv ran back to his room and looked high and low for any kind of message from his man of magic. That's when he noticed the blinking light on the telephone thingy. He pushed the playback key and immediately heard the voice of his Merlin.

"Highness, when you get this message, I'll be hiding out at the La Quinta Hotel out in Walnut Creek. It's too much to explain in a message, but I'm in serious trouble and I need your help. Don't tell anyone else where I am, I mean anyone! You can call my room," and he left a phone number.

King Irv's first thought was that Hershel was somehow a part of the brewing debacle he'd just witnessed on the television screen. He immediately dialed the number. Hershel answered on the first ring in a guarded voice, "Who is it?"

"It's me, King Irv," the monarch replied in a soft, pleasant tone. "So are you in trouble with these Vikings? Did you go into hiding because you knew the police were coming for them?" the king queried. "Do we need to mount a rescue effort for you as well?"

There was silence on the line for almost a minute before Hershel answered. "Worse than that, highness, some American girl is trying to get me to marry her. She wants to go back to England with me... But she doesn't know anything about us or how we got here. I'm terrified! I even traded in my rental Fiat for some kind of Ford thing."

"Well, Verne and I are back now," King Irv soothed. "We're at the Motel 8, and it looks like all hell is about to break loose up at the farm. You'd better get back here as soon as you can and pick us up. I'll make sure no American girl can get her hands on you."

"Oh, thank you, highness. I'll be there in thirty or forty minutes, as soon as I pay my bill here."

"Highness," the man shouted when King Irv, who was waiting in the parking lot of the Motel 8, came over to the dark blue Ford Focus Hershel was driving, "Why didn't you tell me sooner that you were back? I knew that we had some problems up at the ranch 'cause that Darlene woman showed up there a couple days ago, but I was hiding out from Melissa. I was desperate, highness."

As soon as Hershel parked the new car, he and King Irv rushed to Jules Verne's room, pounding furiously on the man's door and shouting for him to wake up and open up. It seemed like hours before they got a response, and then it was just a sleepy "W's it?"

"Now!" Irv shouted, "You must open up right now... And turn on that television thingy. Everything is falling apart and I need your magic right *now*."

Jules Verne came to the door in a frilly white robe with a purple Fleur de Lis embroidered on the breast pocket. "What is all this shouting?" he barked through a sleepy face. "What time is it, anyway?"

"Too late," Irv bounced back at him. "We have to act *right now*." Hershel, behind the King's left shoulder, nodded his agreement.

"Oh, please, your highness. Just calm down for a minute and tell me why you have your knickers in such a twist."

King Irv pointed at the man's television screen, which was now showing uniformed officers trudging down the small rise from State Highway 116 to the farm where Thor and his men crouched in the large wooden barn with make-shift weapons drawn. One or two Vikings appeared to have regained their swords and shields. The voice-over announcer was saying something about a tip from a college student claiming to be the fiancée of Darlene Shacly, that his betrothed had been kidnapped by men from some sort of cult of Viking worshippers.

"Do you have some sort of magic to turn the clock back an hour or so?" Irv hollered at the Frenchman. "Or you?" he added, turning to Hershel.

"Well, there is my time machine," Verne chuckled. "You'll remember that we left it up the street at the brewery last night."

"Then let's get to it right now." Irv shouted. "We must arrive up at that farm before all these police and sheriffs get there and stop this battle thing … nip it in the bud."

"One of the first tenants of time travel," Verne began, "is the rule of causality. We are forbidden to do anything that might change the course of history…"

King Irv grabbed the Frenchman by the throat and began to shake him. "This part of history we are obligated to change, no matter what this causality thing of yours says. We can not let Thor and his men be brought back to jail. It is my sworn duty to get them out of this future time and back to their own place in history."

Jules Verne stared at King Irv, blinked rapidly for a moment or two and mumbled, "Understand." Hershel added, "I think I have a spell or two that we can try along with whatever Jules has in mind."

With that, they all dressed quickly in modern outfits and rushed to the Metaphysical Brewery. The pub itself was closed, but Verne's time machine was right there in the back parking lot where he'd left it.

"Do you want me to go directly to some time before this police raid, like say, last night?" Verne inquired. "Or shall I just go there right here and now?"

"Let's try for right now," Irv shouted. "We'll assess the situation and decide just what we need to do."

"But there's three of us," Verne puzzled. "I don't know if my machine can carry all three of us."

"Then we'll quickly find out, won't we?" King Irv roared as he squeezed into the cockpit of the small contraption behind Verne and Hershel.

When Jules Verne's machine arrived at the farm, they landed in the middle of some kind of bizarre war across the centuries. Armed riot cops were assembling to face off against primitive warriors in animal skins and wooden shields. One or two Vikings waved broad swords and steel hammers. The rest of the men brandished pitchforks, rakes and shovels. They all stood with an air of confidence that they could take any comer. The sheriff's men were assembled on the ridge overlooking the farm. While they were armed to the teeth with modern weapons, they didn't exude such confidence. Quite frankly, they were terrified of these crazy primitives that appeared so sure of themselves. In the loft above the barn's doors, Bird the Cat sat back on his haunches watching the scene below, his ginger tail slowly tracing circles in the air.

The local sheriff sat in his car, a large Dodge Challenger with armor plating, talking with the Sheriff of Alameda County and one of the California State Senators. The local sheriff didn't want to harm these crazy Viking people, and he kept saying so, but the State Senator told him that an all-out attack would be best for the people of this great state. They had to put these crazies in their place, even if it meant slaughtering them all. He didn't mention to the sheriff that he was losing ground in the upcoming election and needed something like a victory against this strange faction in order to hold onto his office.

CHAPTER FORTY-TWO

Inside the barn, Darlene was following Bjorn around like a lost puppy. While Bjorn still fancied her, he had other things on his mind at the moment and was a little perturbed to have some woman from the future constantly clinging to him. Norwegian women didn't cling like this. They fed the cattle and did the chores and saw to the children when their men were away at sea. Certainly Darlene was a good looking girl, but she was not the only good looking girl out there. Bjorn was getting just a little fed up with all her attention. He tried to tell her, but this silly girl didn't seem to understand a word of Norwegian. How could anyone survive in this world if they couldn't speak Norwegian?

Bjorn was just getting settled in away from this Darlene woman when a loud clabber of noise erupted from the hillside beyond their hideaway. Loud pops, like bullets, although no one from Thor's Viking ship's company would know what those were, filled the air outside their hideaway. Some boards in their barn suddenly sported holes and other boards burst inward at them.

When they looked outside, men in khaki uniforms with sticks that sprouted fire came charging down the hill toward their little hideaway. None of these attackers held up Viking style shields and nobody waved a sword. This was such a bizarre attacking force, like nothing they had ever seen.

Thor and a handful of his followers picked up their swords, shields and other weapons, threw open the barn doors and started slowly up the rise toward the modern lawmen. The deputies immediately retreated back to their Humvees and SUVs, where they quickly donned riot gear, pulling on helmets with face masks and picking up bullet-proof Plexiglass shields of their own. Thor and his men watched the show from the barn's large open portal. Bird the cat viewed it from a window in the hay loft above.

The armor clad men regrouped when everyone had their gear on and once again came flying down the slope from the highway. They chased Thor's men back from the opening and burst into the barn. One man knocked Lars down and sat on his back, grabbing the Viking's left arm, ready to throw the steel ring of a cuff on his wrist. Another deputy tackled Bjorn, knocking him forward into the straw covered floor. In an instant, Darlene was on the deputy's back, pounding her fists into his neck and shoulders.

Then, suddenly, the attackers appeared to freeze in mid charge. They moved neither forward or in retreat. It was as if time had stopped. Thor's men held their positions for a moment or two and then relaxed. Some of the men scratched their heads. Others looked around. Those who had been exposed to Christian beliefs crossed themselves and mumbled prayers.

On the hill overlooking the scene, Hershel and Jules Verne congratulated each other on a quickly devised spell, then put their heads together once more for a second, more complicated conjure involving Verne's teleportation idea. King Irv called to his cat and Bird leaped down from the loft, ran forward and jumped to land on his shoulder. Irv, his cat and Verne loaded themselves back into the Frenchman's time machine as Hershel waved his hands about and mumbled some ancient Hebrew phrases.

When the deputies came alive again, they were alone on this distant piece of farm land. There were no Vikings. There was also no time machine and no ginger cat. Only Darlene Shacly remained, arms around the neck of one of the deputies in a strangle hold as she perched on the man's back.

Verne's time travel contraption shimmered back to life on the narrow wharf at the Alameda Marina, where a large pleasure yacht had just morphed back into a very old Viking long boat, complete with very confused crew. Hershel turned to the Frenchman.

"Thanks for all you help. I don't know what we might have done without you." Hershel hesitated a second, then stepped forward and threw his arms around Jules Verne to give him a solid hug. When they separated, the Merlin said, "You know where we are in time and space if you ever want to come for a visit... Or if I can be of any assistance with questions about time, or space... Or even casting spells."

The Merlin quickly turned away to hide the tears forming in his eyes. Verne called after him. "This has been a memorable experience. I don't know if I shall ever dare write about it, but I won't soon be forgetting these adventures we shared."

With a quick wave, King Irv and Hershel scrambled aboard, Thor taking a head count while Hershel headed for his own time travel box, now easy to find at the base of the ship's mast.

Although the Merlin hadn't been successful in repairing his time box, he still had the small sea shell in his pocket that had successfully activated the thing once before. He mumbled words of magic in a sort of Hebrew prayer as he jammed the small mollusk into the hole where his adjusting dial had once rested.

Before Hershel could twist the shell, he heard Thor shout, "Wait a minute. We have one too many Viking sailors here. I believe we've a spy in our midst."

Up by the marina parking area, Alameda police in riot gear spilled out of newly arrived, black painted Humvees in the city parking lot as Hershel jiggled the shell back and forth, up and down. Hershel prayed harder as he continued moving the sea shell about in his time machine. The first law enforcement officer was getting close, almost ready to leap from the pier onto the Viking ship's deck when the long boat finally began to vibrate.

The Alameda officer pitched forward into the cold waters of San Francisco Bay, followed close behind by other policemen with too much momentum to stop. They noted the impression of a hull in the water for a second or two and then it was just a half-dozen heavily armed men in bulky riot gear fighting to stay afloat.

Part IV
Back From the Future

CHAPTER FORTY-THREE

When Hershel looked up from his device, they were once more surrounded by brown water and thick greenery, the very place they had left on that wide muddy river before they landed in San Francisco Bay. He let out a deep moan although he would have been very surprised if they had landed anywhere else, employing just a seashell to tune his machine.

King Irv stood at the ship's rail, where he, too, let out a deep sigh. At least, the monarch thought, I was able to have a few days back with my queen in my own time. Their brief reverie was interrupted by loud shouting.

"A spy, a spy in our midst," Thor was screaming, while farther down the deck a young man in a khaki uniform hollered back that he had been kidnapped. "Where am I?" the man shouted. "What is this desolate place? How do I get back home to Oakland?"

Hershel stepped forward to try and break up the melee. To the young man in the sheriff's uniform, he said, "Sorry, old thing. I guess you might say you've landed yourself somewhere way back in time, no fault of your own. You said you were from Texas? Well, you just might be back home... only a few hundred years earlier than the time you were born."

He then tried to quiet Thor by explaining how the young policeman, who'd been guarding the captured Vikings, had accidentally stepped too close to the teleportation beam moving the Vikings first to the farm and then back to their ship.

Neither man understood or was satisfied by the explanation. They shouted over and around Hershel as he stood there between them. The heated discussion continued until both men were too exhausted to continue, at which time King Irv stepped forward once again to try and explain their situation.

And all the while, Thor's longboat drifted with the current down the wide Mississippi River, back into the Gulf of Mexico. Thor's crew made no effort to land them along the shore. After their experience in San Francisco, everyone was feeling a bit lethargic, and no one could easily forget the wonders they'd seen, or maybe just dreamed in that future world.

Upon reaching the open waters of the Gulf, some of Thor's more senior Vikings began to take an interest once more. No good sailor wanted to be at the mercy of such a large body of water. The decision was made to sail to the right, where they could continue to explore the vast coast of Vinland.

All the while, Hershel spent long hours bent over his time travel box, digging and poking in hopes of finding the problem that kept them traveling between this God-forsaken primitive stretch of Vinland and modern America.

CHAPTER FORTY-FOUR

Back on a south-western course, the Vikings skirted the swampy Gulf coast. Each time they tried to land, go ashore and explore, the area was so wet and mushy that no one was really interested in traipsing far from the shore. Besides that, this area appeared to host even more of those dragon-like lizards that seemed to have a taste for Viking warriors, not to mention snakes that brought death from a single bite to more than one Viking sailor.

Thor's men sailed on. In a week's travel, they came on a pleasant island, a place that would one day be called Galveston, but their explorations around this small slip of land brought them nothing of value, so they put to sea once more.

From there, the coastline curved more toward the south with barrier islands much like Thor and his men had encountered many months before they made the turn around the bend into the Gulf of Mexico.

The Vikings continued to check out every inlet and bay behind these islands as they sailed on to the southwest. Most were shallow areas close to the mainland, but at another wide bay, the Vikings came upon one more group of natives that, to King Irv's delight, also spoke something like Hebrew.

Thor wasn't exactly excited about spending more time here until he discovered that these Cherokee people could replenish his dwindling supply of this new food called potatoes. At King Irv's urging, the Vikings decided to stop here for a few days and grant the Norse sailors a few days of shore leave.

Among the Hebrew colonists known as Cherokees, Hershel discovered a fellow man of magic, Ishtar. Sharing some of the longboat's ale with the man, they quickly formed a bond of friendship.

Ishtar also had some knowledge of magic and the Hebrew Cabala, which he was happy to share with Hershel. They spent a day and a night talking about magic and science, and when Ishtar expressed an interest in time travel, Hershel brought the man down to look at his busted time machine.

Ishtar immediately wanted to know all about how Hershel had come up with the concept of time travel in the first place. With a small piece of charcoal and a large cured goat skin, Hershel sketched the algorithms of his time travel equations, narrating how he came up with the ideas as he covered the large canvas.

When he was finished, Ishtar stared at the goatskin blackboard for a long time before replying. "And you can't make this thing work now?" he inquired.

Hershel went on to describe how the Viking sailor, Burr, had landed flat out on the deck, sending his sword straight into the dial of Hershel's time machine.

Ishtar thought about this for a minute or two, then asked, "Have you tried cleaning out your machine, Hersh?"

"Cleaning?" the Merlin replied, "Like what do you mean?"

"Well," Ishtar answered, "Like cleaning it out to see if there might be a small bit of this chap's sword broken off in there, or something like that."

"Something like that could happen?" Hershel tossed back with a puzzled face.

"Anything can happen," Ishtar chuckled. "You've got to cover all the bases, don't you think?"

Hershel gave back a humble look. "I guess you're right," he told the native man. "And I should have been more astute."

The Cherokee man chuckled back at him. "No harm, no foul," he said. "So, how about we go take a look at this time thingy of yours?"

Ishtar didn't have any more sophisticated tools at his disposal than did Hershel, but the two men of magic approached their problem as best they could. After a thorough examination of the problem, Ishtar told Hershel that he believed the best option was disassembling the machine, taking it right down to the basics, and look at it piece by piece.

The two men of magic spent two days examining Hershel's machine. By the second day of their probe into the mechanism, Thor and his crew were getting anxious to weigh anchor and depart this small harbor, but King Irv was able to stall their departure at least another cycle of the sun.

At dawn of the third day, after Hershel and Ishtar had been working on the problem almost around the clock with very little sleep, Ishtar discovered a tiny bit of rusting iron from the Viking Burr's sword tightly lodged in the mechanism that was shorting out the connection between the crystals. Hershel and his new friend scraped and polished the machine's internal components, reassembled the device and soon had it looking just like new.

Hershel and his king said a heartfelt goodbye to the Cherokee people who had been so helpful to them. King Irv was especially sad to depart from these people whom he felt were almost brothers. What turn of fate had sent them across the broad ocean when his own people had opted for the British Isles? And how had the Diaspora selected where each family of Israel would go and in what direction? Somehow, God must have a plan to spread His truth far and wide across the globe.

By mid day, the Viking longboat was back out on the Gulf and heading southwest once more. And, with news of the time machine being back on line, Thor resumed begging King Irv to demonstrate to his men how the device worked. "You must do this before we can allow you to return home to old England," he told Irv. "My men will want to use this someday." Although Hershel was anxious to try his newly cleaned device, he told King Irv they needed to wait for just the right moment, sometime when Thor and his lieutenants were distracted enough so they could set the controls to take them home to the Wholesale Kingdom without the Vikings suspecting.

CHAPTER FORTY-FIVE

The days became ever more hot and humid as Thor's long-boat sailed southwest along this south-eastern Vinland coast. Viking sailors that dived overboard to bathe in the sea complained that the water seemed much too warm to be refreshing. Thick clouds filled the skies and seasoned seamen griped that they knew something just wasn't right. Those among them of the Christian faith spent many hours in prayer.

Worried about his crew and their safety, Thor sought shelter behind one of the long barrier islands. By the time he'd steered his boat into a broad sheltered bay off the Gulf, the winds were howling a wicked tune through his rigging. The skies turned black as night and the waves climbed higher than the ship's gunnels without respite as heavy rain poured down to set the decks awash. Thor had his men steer deeper into the sheltering harbor, but the high seas followed close on their stern. There seemed to be no escaping this angry surf and pouring deluge, and as the surf grew higher, the wind increased in velocity, driving the rainwater sideways into their faces.

As the last weak sunlight disappeared behind these dark clouds, the raging wind ripped the longboat's sail from its mast and tore loose the men's shields from the ship's gunwales. High water from the bay, combined with that falling from the sky, began to swamp the Viking ship, wave after high wave pouring water over the vessel's low sides. Finally, the mast itself snapped in a forceful gust tossing Hershel's time machine across the roiling deck.

A Viking crew is a hearty lot of men, but some of Thor's fellows began to panic. A number of sailors shed their bearskin tunics, diving over the sides and trying to reach the shore of this shallow bay fighting their way through the unstable flood. They were strong swimmers, but one by one, their heads vanished into the churning foam.

In the midst of this chaos, King Irv with his tunic and breeches torn asunder by the high winds, kept a level head about him. Keeping a low profile as he uncoiled a length of rope from the foredeck, he managed to lash together some boards that the storm had torn loose from the decking.

"Hershel," he cried, "Help me. We must fasten these planks into a platform." His Merlin was still dressed in a modern shirt and a pair of jeans. The jeans were holding up okay, but the shirt hung in tatters around his slim frame.

"Are we building a raft, highness?" Hershel shouted over the howl of the increasing gale, "'Cause I don't think a raft is gonna do well in this choppy stuff."

"Yes and no," his king screamed back, "just give us a hand. And grab your time thingy while you're at it."

"Highness?" Hershel screamed.

"Just do it Hershel!"

The Merlin complied, firmly planting his feet on the canted and slippery deck and hauling his contraption behind him.

By now, King Irv had five wide boards lashed together with still a good length of rope remaining. He wrapped the remaining line around Hershel's time machine as the Merlin brought it onto the makeshift raft. Irv then took a turn around each of their waists with the remaining line, securing them to both time machine and boards.

"Captain," Irv cried out. "Come and join us. We can save you that you might still gain your place in history as a discoverer of these new lands."

"But my men," Thor wailed, "I can't leave my men to these horrid winds and waves. A Captain *must* go down with his ship."

"Suit yourself, Thor," Hershel shouted after him. "But most of them are already doomed to *their* place in history. You still have a chance. Come with us. It's your *true* destiny."

Another wave, the tallest yet, came over the deck of the Viking longboat, lifting the makeshift raft high and then slamming it down just beyond the now breaking-up hull of Thor's vessel. When the foam had settled, Hershel and King Irv found Thor half drowned and clinging to the wreckage of his sinking craft with Bird the cat perched atop his head. Irv managed to get a hold of the Viking captain's shoulder and drag him closer to their small platform of planks.

The king and the Merlin somehow managed to pull Thor aboard with a soaking pile of ginger fur firmly attached to his hair and beard. Hershel quickly set the time machine to bring them to Thor's beloved Hardangerfjord just as the eye of the massive hurricane found them. Bird leaped from the Viking's head onto King Irv's shoulders and in the calm of the storm's center, the small raft began to shimmer and soon it was gone.

CHAPTER FORTY-SIX

They dropped Thor off at his small farm deep in the Norwegian fjord, where the Viking chieftain gave them some thick wool blankets in which to wrap themselves. He then tapped a fresh keg of strong ale that his wife had fetched and invited his friends to dry themselves before the roaring fire in his hearth. Thor's wife also brought some fresh milk for the king's ginger tabby.

Hershel and Irv considered Thor's invitation to spend a few days in his long communal hall. They were exhausted from battling the hurricane out there in the future, but after two pints each of ale and a bowl of a thick, barley gruel, they decided to return to Warehouse castle and their own warm beds.

Hershel once more fiddled with the temporary controls of his rebuilt time box. After some jiggling and poking, he was able to make the necessary adjustments.

When they emerged from their shimmering haze, King Irv, Hershel and Bird paddled their narrow plank raft up onto the pebbles of the narrow North Sea beach just off the Wholesale Kingdom. Although both men were exhausted from their ordeal by the Texas coast, they managed to walk from the beach back to King Irv's castle with the now dry and purring tabby proudly perched on his master's shoulders.

Half way home, they came upon the greenhouse of the Manischewitz Brothers, where they found Ernesto and Julio tending grapes for a brand new batch of wine. Seeing the condition their king and his friend were in, they uncorked a bottle of their special Cabernet for the pair.

"You are a God-send," King Irv told them as he and Hershel polished off their second glass of the rich red wine.

"So where have you guys been?" Julio asked. "We haven't seen you around here in ages."

Hershel started to say something, but King Irv held up a hand to stop him. "You wouldn't believe it if we told you," he chuckled. "Suffice it to say we made a small mistake with Hershel's time invention and we got lost for a while. It was all too much like a bad dream."

The King and his Merlin finished their wine, took a short nap, and by evening, they emerged from the woods by the ninth green of King Irv's golf course just in time for supper at the castle.

Over roast leg of lamb, the king tried to explain to Queen Sophie just where they'd been and what they'd witnessed. Irv's ranting only drew odd looks and rolled-back eyes from Queen Sophie and the castle staff. It seemed as though no time at all had passed since they'd left on the Viking ship to return Princess Judith and her family to modern England. Maybe someday, the good king thought, when Rutherford and Princess Judith came to visit, they could convince his lady that he was not totally bat-shit crazy. After all, Rutherford knew at least something of their strange visit to San Francisco. Bird the maugy gave a brief kitty grin then went back to his cat nap before the fire.

 EPILOGUE

In the distant future, on August 26, 2018, Hurricane Harvey hit the city of Rockport, Texas, on the Gulf of Mexico. The storm surge from Harvey churned up waters all around the area. When the storm had passed, citizens and first responders were surprised to find that Harvey had pushed back the mud and silt in a small expanse of water called Little Bay. Little Bay is a wildlife sanctuary located between the city of Rockport and a small sandbar known as Key Allegro, this narrow strip of sand being host to one of the city's most expensive and exclusive neighborhoods bearing its name, Key Allegro.

First responders and that small handful of people who had remained behind to ride out the storm were met, on Saturday morning, with the sight of an ancient Viking longboat rising slowly from the shallow waters of Little Bay. Its hull was cracked open and its mast was broken, lying to one side, but its dragon-headed prow rose proudly from the oyster beds of Little Bay.

It was unclear how word had spread so quickly, but within three days, archaeology students from the University of Oslo were camped in the nearby Coastal Oaks Preserve, wading into the shallow bay to study the well preserved timbers of the old long boat. One of their professors journeyed to Austin with a request from the Norwegian government that they might exhume the old wreck and transport it back to Norway where the vessel could join similar artifacts in the university's Museum of Cultural History on Bygdøy, an island in Oslo Harbor.

All the Texas government asked was for the Norwegians to avoid any publicity. It had to be understood that American academia would still steadfastly cling to the party line that no European had touched our shore before Christopher Columbus.

And so before electricity or water were restored to the Rockport community, before the bulk of residents returned and before the media looked any closer than damaged and destroyed property, the Norwegian government brought a small unmarked ship into Fulton Harbor with a crew of Norwegian Special Forces who were able to crate up the remains of Thor's ship, quite possibly the first Norwegian vessel ever to reach the coast of Texas, and bring it home, not to its original port in Hardangerfjord, but at least close by in the Oslo Fjord.

In Oxford, England, the now retired-to-the-future King Irv and Queen Sophie watched some rare BBC footage of the Norwegian rescue effort, film which was never released in America. Irv placed his hand over Sophie's and turned a smile her way. "You don't know how close Hershel and I came," he winked. "That hurricane was one hell of a storm."

ABOUT THE AUTHOR

S koot Larson is a native Los Angelino, a musician, music critic and a Viet Nam veteran. He has also worked as a disc jockey, actor, speech therapist, stand-up comedian, behavioral counselor and streetcar conductor. His previous works include the Lars Lindstrom Zen-Jazz Mystery series, a black-humor novel about health care in America entitled "Apollo Issue," and a political humor novel, "The Palestine Solution, and the King Irv fantasy series" Skoot lives with his two cats, Miles and Dexter, in Rockport, Texas.

Made in the USA
San Bernardino, CA
30 May 2018